The cast of characters in *The Big Empty* are mostly young and eager but unfulfilled in a modern world that offers little. Yet through the grotesquerie of latent violence, real terrible violence, bad sex, not bad sex, drink besotted and drug-crazed efforts to connect with a life, Dillon draws humanity out of the most unpromising circumstances.

"fresh and spiky with warmth and truth . . . a Coatbridge Dubliners*"*   Edwin Morgan

Des Dillon was born and brought up in the Lanarkshire town of Coatbridge. He works as a teacher of English and as a writer.

THE BIG EMPTY

other books by the author:
Me & ma Gal (1995)

THE
BIG
EMPTY

A COLLECTION
OF
SHORT STORIES

DES DILLON

Argyll
publishing

First published 1997
Argyll Publishing
Glendaruel
Argyll PA22 3AE

The author has asserted his moral rights.

All characters and situations in this book are entirely fictional.
Subsidised by the Scottish Arts Council

THE SCOTTISH ARTS COUNCIL

Acknowledgement is made to Buckfast Abbey, Devon for
cover illustration permission.

British Library Cataloguing-in-Publication Data.
A catalogue record for this book is available from the
British Library.

ISBN 1 874640 08 4

Origination
Cordfall Ltd, Glasgow

Printing
Caledonian International
Book Manufacturing Ltd, Glasgow

For Bonzo, Davy and Danny

Midway this way of life we're bound upon,
I woke to find myself in a dark wood,
where the right road was wholly lost and gone.

Dante

Acknowledgements

Some stories in this collection have appeared in other publications and have been broadcast. Paddy Cox first appeared in *Campus Magazine* (1995). Bunkers & Doors is a story from a body of work which was published as the novel, *Me & ma Gal*. *Me & ma Gal* was serialised as a BBC Radio Scotland *Storyline* in April 1996. Bunkers & Doors is also part of the filmscript, *Itchycooblue*. The Dummy was shortlisted for *Prime Cuts* – STV short films. Our Lady of the Carmels was broadcast on BBC Radio Scotland in October 1996. Any Old Summer is from an unpublished novel, *Bright Brand New Day* written in 1985. Disintegration was first published in *West Coast Magazine* (1997).

Contents

Paddy Cox

Paddy Cox walked wi one arm out an limped like crazy.
The weans used to take the piss out him. *Paddy Cox, nose
like a fox, it's the way he walks, cos he's got the pox,* they'd go.
He had red hair disappearin off his head. There was always
scabs on his head standin out there against the red skin.
The weans used to give him pennies for throwin stones up
in the air an headerin them. The wee bastards. He was just
an animated toy to them. The blood wasn't real. The
screams mixed in wi their laughter. Paddy Cox would stand
there, his big blue eyes like Frankenstein when he can't
understand why people are treatin him like this.

Instead of sayin W, Paddy Cox always says B. And
instead of J, he said D. So a wall becomes a ball and a walk

becomes a balk; a jockey becomes a dockey and jam becomes dam. He always had a bench to himself at mass did poor Paddy. He slept rough in the closes of the Slap Up. His mother, God bless her soul, had died. There was no-one to take him in. No-one to put his clothes on and keep him clean. And ye can't live on the wind so people used to take turns at feedin him. He was a sorry sight. No wonder he had a row all to himself at twelve o clock mass.

There was this Sunday and these Missionary Fathers came to St Augustine's. Paddy Cox was in the row behind me. He always sat facin straight on to the Sacred Heart statue. Through the foggy haze of boredom I could hear one of the Missionaries bumpin his gums all about Jesus an saints an stuff. At the same time Paddy, who usually sat there stock still starin into the compassionate eyes of the plaster statue, was shufflin the old feet, gruntin an gettin restless. And he stank. The movement was sendin waves of sour food and urine through the chapel. On and on this missionary's goin but no-one's listenin cos they're all holdin their breath cos of Paddy Cox.

—We must give more to Jesus and that means hard cash. Prayers are alright. I'm not askin yees to stop the prayin nor nothin. Keep on prayin. Pray all the more but these poor starvin people they need your money. Think how lucky yees all are to have a roof over yer heads an a job in the steelworks n mines. These people . . . they've got to eak their little livin out the land . . . land that's baked hard or deep wi mud. They roam around and sleep under trees. Dig into yer pockets. Think of them when yer sat in yer cosy little single-end there wi the fire blazin away an the kettle on an all the weans snug there in the bed. Imagine you didn't have that job to feed them weans. No matter what we think there's always that bit more we can offer.

Ye'd've thought we had a good life to hear him. I was nearly convinced maself till I thought of the six o clock start an the twelve hour shifts in the dry black dust of Dundyvan. New steel hot as hell. Christ, I was nearly convinced till I thought of the nine weans all stuffed into the box bed an me an her on a roll out mattress on the floor. Christ . . . It was makin me mad so it was. Livin in the Slap Up amongst the knives an the head butts an the whorin an the drinkin an the dyin weans an the dyin men an the mournin wummin an the constant glow of gas lamps through the smog. Oh ay, I was fuckin glad alright.

—Good to be alive. Desus Mary an Doseph look after us!

Everyone looked round and there's the Saint Vincent de Paul passkeepers usherin Paddy Cox out the chapel.

—Div more to Desus. Div more, div all yous got. Be've got to div more to Desus.

Paddy screamed all the way out the doors. Ye could feel the cold blast of air and then the doors closed. The Missionary was obviously disgusted by the outburst and resumed his pleadin for compassion and mercy.

When we left the mass Paddy was sittin shiverin in the snow. Some people drew him black looks but most ignored him and carried their Sunday serenity back into the high black walls of the Slap Up. When the priest shut the chapel doors Paddy shuffled into the arches out of the reach of the sleet. The last I saw him he's curled up and snortin warm air into the cold January sky.

—Be must div more to Desus.

He rocked to sleep murmurin to himself most nights so I suppose that's what he done here.

I go home an get ma tea. The weans are runnin riot so I goes out into Turner Street just to see what's what. I'm standin in the close out the sleet smokin, when I sees this red/pink figure runnin crazy out of the storm.

There's a gang of weans, none of them mine, thank Christ, runnin after the figure. He's screamin an moanin and the shrill cries of the weans crack off all the buildings.

People come to windows.

I remain immobile. It's Paddy Cox an he's stark ravin naked. His cock's bouncin from thigh to thigh and it seems strange that he's got one . . . that he's a man . . . that he's a real fuckin man . . . Paddy Cox's balls . . . I'm standin there but I can't believe it. Snowballs are hurlin at him ten a penny and they're explodin off his tight skin. He's screamin so loud and painfully ye can see all his back teeth an ye're thinkin he's goin to burst right through his skin any minute . . . he's goin to burst right through his fuckin skin. He looks to me for help as he passes – his eyes are all whites and screamin.

HELP HELP.

I can't do nothin. I lowers the head, ashamed. I can't even stop the weans peltin him they're too far gone in a frenzy.

The snow on the cobbles is slush an his feet are black an he slips an gets back up every few steps. His mother would be turnin in her grave. They're kickin him an their

Maws are whistlin from the windows an throwin things. There's blood in the snow from his knees and his hands an there's blood on his body where the razor cold snow has sliced the skin. He's writhin but still movin up Turner Street . . . up to the top of the hill where a gang of men, red eyed from drinkin, have gathered wi their belts off and unrolled. The black leather and the buckles shine. Paddy Cox sees them and drops to his knees. He looks up to the sky. The sleet is whinnyin down and stickin in his face. The crowd of men surge forwards. Their eyes are pickin out bare flesh to hit.

—Our Fader hoo art in hivin,

Paddy starts prayin. The weans are round him now, dancin in a circle and singin their song.

—Paddy Cox nose like a fox it's the way he walks cos he's got the pox Paddy Cox nose like a fox it's the way he walks cos he's got the pox Paddy Cox nose like a fox it's the way he walks cos he's got the pox Paddy Cox nose like a fox it's the way he walks cos he's got the pox Paddy Cox nose like a fox it's the way he walks cos he's got the pox

They're scuddin him wi hard ice snowballs on the sound of Cox, Fox, Walks and Pox. The men are breakin through the dancers.

—We'll show ye ya pervert bastard prancin about like that wi our weans.

The men are rollin up their sleeves an spittin on the ground an movin in for the kill.

Oh my God he's dead, I thinks an I'm movin at top rate into the dancers . . . through them . . . Paddy Cox is still Our Fatherin away there an I'm on big Joe Brennan. I lunges low on the way in. The steel on the soles of ma boots slides along the cobbles. All the weans look round in time to see me spring up from a half shut knife position and stick the head right into Brennan's face. The crunch rung up every close. I hold onto him cos we're goin forward and down. I let him go an rip the belt out his hand. Blackout. A big Polis had crunched me on the head and piled a few of us into the black Maria.

The next mornin we're all up in front of The Beak. It turns out that Paddy Cox had got into St Augustine's, took all his clothes off and folded them neatly on the altar. When he came out the weans seen him and chased him up the street.

—Do you have anything to say for yourself Mister Cox? goes the Judge. Paddy's standin there in a suit a mile too big for him. The Polis an public are laughin. We're strainin to hear what he's got to say from the cells. I can see the side of his head over the dock. He looks up wi pitiful eyes. His head is scabbed up where the weans got him wi ice.

—I . . . I . . .

—Speak up Mister Cox I can't hear you, drones the judge like he's the Pope of Rome.

—I . . . I . . . dey said div more to Desus . . . div more to Desus . . . ma tlothes . . . I only hid ma tlothes . . . Dave thim to Desus . . . put thim on the altar . . . Desus'll div thim ti thi poor black weans . . . keep thim warm . . . div more thi said . . . div more to Desus.

The court went silent. Through the bars on ma cell I could see the sky darken.

Jerry and Danya

There's me an Wullie an Carmen in this Blackpool bedsit. We're drinkin a couple a bottles an there's a load a Supers an Callies. Me an Wullie's been doin some bare-fist boxin an Carmen's been flickin her hair an chain-smokin. We're well bruised an stinkin wi sweat. We're sittin there tellin stories about the old days to impress Carmen. All that mind-the-time shite.

I'd boost him up; he'd boost me up.

—Mind the time I came into your house Wullie an ye're standin there wi yer Maw pressed up agin the wall an a knife at her throat? I says.

Wullie laughs an goes —Ay, an ye turned round an walked right back out again.

He laughs loud as fuck this time an nods the head thon way so I'll go back to the start of the story. Carmen drags the fag an swings her head like a plastic doll to Wullie an back to me.

She goes —You had yer mother up against the wall wi a knife?

Her mouth's wide an her top lip's curled. Wullie takes a good swig out the bottle.

—Ahhhhh, he says. —I was a right crazy bastard when I was young. Nat right, he goes to me.

—Never out the jail, says I.

—Fuckin mental, he says lookin to me.

—A right crackpot, I goes.

Kshhh. Carmen crashes another Super an puts her fag out *wshsht* in the old one.

Wullie's squeezin some plooks.

He looked like Oliver Reid did Wullie.

—Who do I look like? I mean who the fuck do I look like, tell they cunts who I look like! he'd always go.

—Oliver Reid Wullie . . . ye look the dead spit of Oliver Reid ma man, we'd say an that's him happy for the rest of the night. Spotty bastard.

There's the three of us well oiled. I'm about to launch into this story . . . when . . .

clump

clump clump

clump

. . . there's these big footsteps on the stairs. We thought it was the Polis cos we were up to all sorts. Carmen swings the black curls nippin Wullie's eye. She gives me the big brown I'm-terrified-of-the-Polis eyes an I looks to Wullie cos he's an experienced jailbird.

The door bursts open an in bounces Slither. We all sighs an laughs. There's fags sparkin up all over the place an cunts are crashin open cans left right an centre. Slither smiles – bleached hair, red face an clothes threatening to burst if she lets her breath out. I mind her cleavage flattened in by this tight white shirt thing.

—Hi babe, says Wullie cos she's his bird. Deft as fuck she plants a slabbery, says hiya honey, lights a fag, picks up a can an *kshhh* she's pourin it down her neck.

I was goin to clap her for professional alcoholism when I hears . . .

sob sob sob boo hoo

sob sob sob boo hoo sob sob sob boo hoo sob sob sob boo hoo sob sob sob boo hoo

coming from out in the lobby. I gives Slither the question mark eyes.

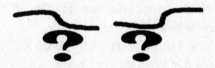

She shakes the head an throws a sympathetic thumb over her shoulder.

—It's Danya, she says as if she's been skelped by a car.

—What about Danya? I asks.

—That bastard Jerry.

Wullie jumps wi the fightin head on.

—Has he done her in again . . . I telt him the last time . . .

—Sit down Wullie, goes Slither, shovin him back in the chair wi one hand.

Her big arse is scuffin ma cheek everytime she turns. Carmen can't see I'm enjoying it. Ye can just see the printed flowers on her knickers cos she's wearing white ski pants. I'm takin in the flowers so I'm not giving two fucks about Danya greetin all over the carpet.

She knew what she was doin did Slither. She knew that big arse was a turn on, specially wi the wee flowery knickers diggin in. Wullie's lookin all concerned cos it was Slither's pal greetin an Carmen's too young to notice the wee strokes bein pulled all round her. She's believin all this concern-for-a-fellow-human-being shite. I knew what Slither was into. This is a chance she's not missin. She rubs the thigh tight across ma shoulder this time.

Danya gets coaxed into the room sobbing.

FLOP

she goes on the couch. Carmen shuffles off all important like to make a wee cup a tea.

—There Danya don't worry about it . . . says Wullie an squeezes her knee an pats her shoulder. Slither's too busy facing me an stretching so I can see the front of her knickers an the old pubes lookin right at me.

Shag me,

they're sayin.

Shag me baby.

It's about four inches away an fuck me, it's pulsin . . . no kiddin.

—What d'ye take in yer tea? Carmen shouts in from the scullery. —What d'ye take in yer tea Danya luv? says Slither in her Blackpool accent. Danya looks into Slither's eyes like the Madonna but she can't say nothin an gives it Niagara Falls again. Slither cuddles the top of her body an Wullie gives the thigh a good squeeze.

—Aw the poor darlin . . . Give her milk an two sugars then! Slither shouts.

In comes the tea an Slither gives us the story.

—That pig Jerree. Ee should be bloody shot. D'ye know what he's gone an done?

We all nod left an right like fuckin puppets. She's doin well walking up an down by the window. I'm getting a double deal here. I'm gettin the gossip an an eyeful of Slither's body. She's struttin it well.

—Ee took her to the Noggin. They got their Giros today so they went to the pub after they got the food in. Everything was OK, nothin amiss . . . they were getting on better that usual.

—Nat right Luv? She goes to Danya.

Boo HOO Hoo,

goes greetin face. Slither taps her back an Wullie's hand's gettin further up the thigh.

—Anyway, who comes in but that big Jimmy the Bite

an Jerry's speaking wi im up the bar. But Danya thinks all the whispering's about dope. Jimmy's the Man in the Noggin now. Can ye imagine it . . . what a sight that skinny runt Jerry an fat Jimmy the Bite; Laurel and fookin Ardy.

Danya nearly laughs at this bit but then

sob sob

she goes an drops the head back into her hands.

Slither gives her of couple of seconds.

—So. The Bite vanishes an it's an all day job; pool the lot . . . great day. They've got a good drink in them. Jerry leans over an kisses Danya an if that don't surprise her, he asks her to go home an make one of them apple pies that he loves.

sob sob sob boo hoo

sob sob sob boo hoo sob sob sob boo hoo sob sob sob boo hoo sob sob sob boo hoo Waaaaaaaaaaaaaaaaaaaaaaaaa!!!!!!!!!

Danya cries for real this time like she was holding in a vomit an out it comes. Fuck me she could strip woodchip wi that voice. Aretha Franklin she's not. Wullie pulls her into his chest. His hand's still on her thigh. Slither goes on.

—Danya skips home all happy that Jerry wants one of her pies . . . an she's bloody good at making them. The guy in Snappy Bite wanted to buy them by the undred, nat right doll?

sob sob sob boo hoo
sob sob sob boo hoo sob sob sob
boo hoo sob

—It's a blinkin sin. Well don't three hours pass an no Jerry. Danya phones the Noggin an George tells her Jerry's left just after her wi Jimmy the Bite . . . Scotch Git. She's just put the phone down an it rings again. It's Jerry.

—Got that apple pie ready yet? the bastard says.

—Yes Jerry. It's been ready for ages. Is Jimmy the bite coming up for some too? says the poor lass.

sob sob sob boo hoo

—Ya stupit cunt, he goes. Well! – she can't believe her ears.

Jerry?

Want to hear what that Scotch bastard says?

We all nod wi open mouths. I'm tryin hard as fuck not to laugh.

—See you ya ugly bastard . . . I widn't feed your pies to a pig . . . force it down yer throat an die. D'ye know where I am stupit?

The Noggin?

The NOGGIN . . . the fuckin NOGGIN? Naw . . . I'm no in the fuckin Noggin . . . ya daft cunt . . . I'm in ma mammies . . . she's made me an apple pie . . . listen can ye hear me eating it . . .

Ees got the cheek to slabber an munch down the phone; one of his moother's pies. He gives it to poor Danya . . . —I'm sorry I ever married you ya English slut . . .

I never hit ye hard enough the last time . . . I should've kilt ye.

An there he is . . . up in Glasgow an eating this other apple pie over the phone at Danya.

There's no stopping Danya now.

Waaaaaaaaaaaaaaaaaaaaaaaaaaaaaaa

The tears are dripping onto the roofs of the Super Lagers at her feet. She doesn't want a drink. She wants Jerry an that puzzles me how she'll still take him back after all the doins an dirty tricks he's pulled.

—Wullie have you got petrol in yer car? Slither asks.

—Ye want me to take her all the way to Coatbridge?

—Well it's just bloody right aint it?

Wullie's not wanting to go. He's been drinkin all day an wants to batter on. But he's no match for the bold Slither – she goes for his soft spot.

—I want you to go up wi Danya an if that prick so much as touches her the wrong way you kick his fookin cunt right in.

Wullie loved that. Out comes the chest wi the car keys. He gets up an starts loading drink into a carrier. That's when Slither pulls the trump card.

—Carmen, she goes, mind how you wanted to go to Glasgow an get some more clothes?

Carmen jumps up. Yes . . . yes. She's clapping her hands like a twelve year old. Slither's arse brushes into ma face.

—An it'd be better for a girl to keep Danya company, Carmen. Be a doll!

Me an Slither wave them up the street. Off ye pop, there they go, a couple of days in bonnie Scotland. Back in the flat I'm in ma chair thinking how to make The Move on Slither. Christ, in she comes, locks the door an starts to undress. I can feel her breath on the back of ma neck an I can hear Wullie's exhaust rattlin up Lytham Road.

Mushrooms an Spaceships

Me an Bonzo were over Kerrs park this Sunday night birlin on the magic mushrooms. We're out our fuckin heads man – solid gone – away wi the bongos. He's dossin about twenty feet in front of me all the time an goin whooheee an all this mad stuff. He's spinnin round an lookin up at the stars an ye can see he's havin some trip. His arms are out an his fingertips are in constant collision wi the cold air. He's a helicopter an he's screwin himself up the sky into the stars. He's solid gone an he's lovin it.

But this night I've went all contemplative. I've got the Universe? what it's all about? why are we here? an all that shite tumblin through ma head like a mad washin machine an I can't shake it off.

—Zanussi – tell – me – what – this – life – is – all – about,
I'm chantin.
—Zanussi – tell – me – what – this – life – is – all – about.
Laughin.
—Zanussi – tell – me – what – this – life – is – all – about.
Chantin.
—Zanussi – tell – me – what – this – life – is – all – about.
Laughin.
—Zanussi – tell – me – what – this – life – is – all – about.
Chantin.
—Zanussi – tell – me – what – this – life – is – all – about.
Laughin.

An sometimes Bonzo likes to talk about philosophy an planets an stuff. An sometimes he likes to swing on trees an shout out loud. This is a shout out loud night. This night he's spinnin out on the football fields an he's on his own. Ye can hear his feet scrunchin in the red ash – every time he spins it sounds like a shootin star. An I sees one whizzin over the pitch in sparks an clouds of dust an clashin an splodin on the wire mesh fence.

He's out there in his own solar system. He's untouchable. He doesn't even notice the crazy glint of the young team's wine bottles arcin through the darkness. They're hidin among the swings an stuff cos me an the bold Bonzo – we come wi a bad reputation. Mad as fuck. No cunt in their right mind's goin to mess wi us specially when

29

we're out our face on mushies.

I walks past the young team. I've got the black tammy on. I call it the don't-fuck-wi-me hat. They go all quiet an still except for the sudden glow of a fag flarin in October winds.

By this time the Captain's out the other end of the ash park. He's singing Floyd out dead loud.

MOTHER DO YOU THINK THEY'LL DROP THE BOMB?

I jogs up to him.

BOOM!!!!

he shouts.

MOTHER DO YOU THINK THEY'LL DROP THE BOMB?

I looks at his face.

BOOM!!!!

he shouts.

MOTHER DO YOU THINK THEY'LL DROP THE BOMB?

I tries to talk to him.

BOOM!!!!

he shouts.

MOTHER DO YOU THINK THEY'LL DROP THE BOMB?

I goes all quiet. Ye can hear the ants crawling in the red ash.

BOOM!!!!

he shouts then goes all quiet too.

We walk through Rosehall school. He says nothin but I know he knows ma head's doin overtime on the Universe question.

He gives it,

—*we don't need no education we don't need no education we don't need no education we don't need no education we don't need no education we don't need no education.*

Over an over so that if ye looked in the school windows ye could see rows an rows of weans scribblin away bowed down in front of the marchin teacher. Ye could even hear the pencils on the paper even though all the rooms were empty an the windows were made out of this criss crossed perspex stuff ye can't see though.

To put ye in the picture. When ye're on the mushies or acid or somethin like that – hallucinogenics – ye feel like some great revelation is a brain cell away. Like ye suddenly can pronounce a word in a new fuckin way an the key to God's Shoppin Mall appears hangin there in the air right in front of yer eyes.

—Is that a fuckin key that floats afore me?

It's all Lego Bucketland stuff but I'm right into searchin out the truth behind it. The truth's there if ye can find yer way in – God; The Universe; The Meanin of Life – the whole fuckin shebang.

This night I'm into searchin for The Truth more than ever but Bonzo's into spinnin an splodin bottles off the wall. They look like the Big Bang to me but to him they're packets of violence. Physical emotion.

Boosh. Boosh. Boosh.

Three bottles one after the other crash an a percussion of

glass transforms to star shrapnel falling on the black tarmac of forever.

I grabs his arm an he presses right close to me. It's not like we're gay nor nothin.

—Right what the fuck's it all about this time, he says in a quiet voice lookin to the sky. I tries to explain.

—Bonzo, I goes . . . I'm goin to get right inside this thing to see what it's all about.

He hits me wi the usual shrug an palms out, —What do ye want to go an do that for? It's all about what it's all about.

I'm rubbin ma chin like them intellectuals do. He's starin at me through the new silence waitin sedately for ma answer.

—No . . . but I'm going right inside it to see what the fuck's goin on in there . . . there's somethin happenin . . . it's big an I want to see what it's all about. I want . . . I want . . . The Truth.

He nods twice exactly wi his mouth open.

—The truth is; we pick em, we take em, we birl, we smoke a joint, we go home to bed. We do what we do, we see what we see, we love it or hate it, we eat our piece, we catch the bus home an our wifes give us the *where-have-you-been-all-fuckin-day* routine an we don't get a shag till mornin when they're dyin for it, then we do it all over again next Friday.

I've picked up a star an it's buzzin between ma forefinger an thumb. I stares into it, talkin.

—I know that Bonzo, but there's somethin else in there . . . somethin that words can't get a grip on. Somethin that tells ye the whole shebang. Somethin that's bigger than God an the whole fuckin sideshow.

—Aw fuck off. I just take them an get a buzz an that's that. What's the point in analysin? That only does yer head in that kind of thinkin. Look what it done to Foggy – he thought hisself onto the end of a rope an a wardrobe up at the door an a mad fuckin bible floatin in a pool of pish below his legs. No fuckin thank you. I'll stick to spinnin round an shoutin out loud as fuck.

—D'ye know what that's like Bonzo? I goes, stickin ma hands on ma hips.

He stops whooeein an looks at me. —No what is it like? he goes.

—That's like you an me come round this park every Friday night an this spaceship U F fuckin O thing picks us up an takes us for whirl round the Universe an drops us off back here at midnight – an you don't even look out the windies.

He looks. He gets it. He smiles. His teeth are enormous white slabs that are takin over the world. Ye can hear this wooshin noise – it's the noise that white makes an then,

Ha ha ha ha ha ha ha ha Ha ha ha ha ha ha ha ha Ha ha ha ha ha ha ha ha Ha ha ha ha ha ha ha ha Ha ha ha ha ha ha ha ha ha Ha ha ha ha ha ha ha

Any Old Summer

(1986)

The rain came down in a fizzing drizzle as they reached the old bargehouse. They sheltered and watched the downpour in absent-mindedness, eyes out of focus, ears locked on the hissing wetness that was glossing the countryside. The scene was hypnotic. The empty fields, the rain deffracting the world into an abstracted blur. Mick was gone. The trees and the careless horses shone like new wax through the foggy rain. Today, the rains seemed in harmony with the land and the beasts. The soft focus widened his eyes.

A trace of rain dribbled down the gutterings. The birds began to zoom about in force and Stig was off like a swallow. Mick started back to the real world and stepped out onto the muddy path. The path smelled fresh and was highlighted by neat little puddles of fresh rainwater. He stared at the water, grey, with a shaft of blue as the clouds cleared, came back, and cleared again. The water appealed to him. Out of the blue came a powerful craving to drink from the puddles, a thirst like the inside of a steelwork. He moved to a large puddle. He looked into the fresh cold slap of water, licked his lips, and sank to his knees.

Some clouds rolled over the puddle. He put both hands into it slowly so as not to disturb the bottom. He licked his lips and pursed them, put his face in the water scattering his own reflection and sucked the water of the heavens like a man on the edge. The water ran in cool rivulets down his throat parched by a strange and vivid imagination.

Under a thick tree was an old tinker. He stared at the curious youth and his odd dog. A smile shone through the creases. White teeth showed. He stood shaking on the point of laughter. As Mick moved the old man slid into the darkness of the back of the trees. In the shadows.

Mick started up, breathing quick and heavy as he came to his senses. Stig drank on regardless. Mick looked around, he felt he was being watched. No-one. He laughed and wondered what drove men to such impulse.

The noise of Stig lapping at water.

He flung a mock kick at the dog. It dodged to the right and his foot landed in the puddle.

—Shit, he shouted shaking the water from his leg. Stig was grinning from the trees. Mick thought he heard laughing and swung round. Not breathing, he stared hard, scanning the dark areas between trunks. Seeing nothing he shook his head and walked on, pensive.

He found a good stick.

Stig nuzzled round the edge of the shadows. In the trees the sun filtered through and lit up some inner darkness; the heart of the forest. Some places were shining and golden, others black as jet.

The old tinker stalked Mick, his brown face folding and unfolding like a concertina as he giggled at the find. His eyes gathered information, storing it, keeping it. He let out a call like Red Indians do. Mick started. Stig ran to his side. Silence. Pause. They walked on – listening.

The old tinker was joined by two small, dark and partially clothed men. They murmured through the woods and crept onwards, staying within sight of Mick and Stig. Mick could walk for hours on a rainy day that emptied the landscape of people.

The path led to rugged country. He was sure he knew this area; he had surveyed it from the train only a few days before. It all looked different now. It was alien. The trees looked as if they had stood unmoved for all time. Nothing was more inviting in his mind than a piece of land where the trappings of modern town-life were kept to a minimum. So here, it was a thing for him to turn full circle and see; no pylons; no smoke. The air was crisp and clear. There was no railway to be seen, no trains to be heard, no motorway noises. There was nothing to indicate Lanarkshire. He dreamed on.

—Just like the dreams in the classroom . . . Applied Mechanics . . . staring out the window . . . empty spaces looking out over empty spaces . . . dreaming of these spaces in the woods, empty of people. Back . . . back through to that time without pylons . . . where man lived from the land in random fashion . . . nothing changed . . . only the night into day and the day into night . . . that was the clock. There were no lands . . . countries . . . nations . . . no owners of this tree . . . that blade of grass . . . a patch of sky . . . a puddle of clear water.

He laughed at the thoughts welling.

The woods came back into focus on his mind. He wondered how he had been drawn so deep into that thinking. It was impossible to re-trace them back to their starting point.

He had wandered far without checking any landmarks. The path was lost too. Mick became uneasy. He looked over at Stig. He was at ease like he had been in the Highlands, pushing himself through a sea of fallen cones and pine needles. Mick had never seen them so thick. Stig muzzled a cone through a patch until only his tail could be seen sticking up. He moved about like a queer prehistoric animal. An unseen brute. Appearing with his face black as jet he threw the cone at Mick, who threw it violently into a clearing and walked on. Thinking.

A roe deer started as the cone hit it light and silent on the rump. It had been sleeping. A rustle – as Mick's head turned a twig cracked the crystal silence. It was the first wild deer he had seen here. It was bolting for the thickness of the woods. As it reached the edge of safety, an arrow thunked into its side and it crashed, knees bent, breathing hard and heavy. Its eyes stuck out in fear and pain. Death rang out in a silence that cut across Mick's fear. The deer grunted helpless.

Mick stood shocked and still, too scared to run, too scared to hide. He stood just where he was, waiting and watching the deer. Its dying noises racked him. Then, out of the woods, appeared two small men. One held a large, rough knife. Both were dressed in a sackcloth material. The first grabbed the twitching deer. His fingers slid up its nostrils and he jerked its head back. He slid the knife across the throat swift and efficiently, slicing. The blood gushed out, splashing onto itself on the grass. The deer jerked finally, rustling the undergrowth with its thrusting back legs, then lay still and dead. Both men grabbed a hind leg each and dragged it towards the darkness.

Mick heard the low murmurings, quiet and mysterious, dissipate away from him and Stig. He crouched down scared. He waited a long while on the coming of moonlight. Stig curled up beside him and they fell asleep. The moonlight came and went unnoticed. He awoke in the subdued light of morning. His bones ached all over and his eyelashes felt as if they had been knitted together with some fine and tensile spider's web. Stig had worked himself well into the hollow of a tree and was barely visible through the thickness of the undergrowth. The dew shone like baubles on the blades of grass and leaves. It lay on Mick's hair like a fine net. He shook his head from side to side and the water rattled quietly on the surrounding rhododendron leaves. He bent down and hit the dog a slap on the rump. The moisture clouded the air as they moved into the morning fear. Mist gathered and ungathered.

The dawn held an eerie chill about it. Mick thought of Stonehenge on a mist-clad morning. Stig stretched his back and for a moment he looked like a long, sleek, black and white cat. He compressed into shape and bolted in course circles around Mick, wagging excitedly. Mick took little notice as Stig bumped its head into trees sneezing abruptly, then growling as if the tree had run into the dog. He barely registered the snarls as he thought, trying to piece together the events. Although it was light and morning, he could not figure out where he was and which would be the best way out of these woods. He had been sure that he knew every inch of the area. It seemed to him, after thought, that he did not.

The crack of a twig brought silence again. He stood holding his breath. Stig, however, after a momentary pause, downed his ears and carried on diving and tumbling. Mick thought he had seen a figure move into the half-light then back into the dark. Again something shone to shape itself only to fade again in the dark of the woods. He bent down and lifted a good stick. He felt safer with something in his hand. They walked on, the dog to the front, through the clearest parts of the forest where he would have enough room to swing the stick. He gathered in confidence as he walked.

The nature of the scenery had changed. The ground underfoot had become marshy and smelled of peat and loam. Puddles gathered every step or two, some congregating into small lochans, others were small and deep, potholes of unknown depths. The calm water was white and satiny. It made him want to stroke it, to let his skin feel what his eyes saw. He knew this inviting softness would be ruined by a hand bursting the surface.

The trees developed a thin and wispy slant, a gauntness that threw itself up from the acidity. The area looked like a pot of something about to boil over. The land ahead grew luxuriously as rain forest. To his left was a gigantic club moss surrounded by great looming ferns which swayed in the warming breeze. On the firmer ground there were conifers, smaller ferns and horsetail plants like cycads. In the distance great ponderous trees that looked like redwoods.

A fear crawled into him again. He was lost now for sure. Nothing offered him any clue as to his whereabouts, he had no bearings in these lands. Even his homing instinct told him nothing. When they all ventured into new territory in the young days he had been the one they turned to when they felt lost, or hungry. He never had to let them down but now he was scared. He thought he was being watched. In these perplexing woods, something was tracking his movements.

—Why no approach? Are they hostile? Do they fear my hostility? Or are they waiting for the best opportunity to attack?

He gripped the stick much tighter and breathed heavy looking from side to side.

—Are they afraid . . . but still . . . curious enough to track me . . . to watch me . . . where is this place?

His thoughts were interrupted by a cry from above. Stig, for the first time looked afraid. He moved to Mick's side. In the unusually empty sky a huge bird flew. Mick stared in disbelief.

—What's an eagle doing . . .?

His words trailed up into the sky from his tilted head. The Golden Eagle crossed. It exuded power and control. Its long wings stretched out as it glided. The tips of the wings spread out like reaching fingers, feeling the wind. It flew in a pattern of alternate swoops and glides, deep swoops that showed its underneaths. The ground in front twitched and brought to view, a blue hare. It knew there was an eagle in the sky.

The eagle came crashing down, deafening, through the trees, with its lethal talons stretched out in front of the powerful body. Stig growled. Close, it had looked Mick straight in the eye, alighting then with the writhing hare squealing hopeless in the crushing talons. He had seen its piercing eyes and prominent brows. Soaring up with each steady beat of its wings, the eagle gave a cry and turned off into a silent sky. Absolute silence. Then things began to stir in the brush and trees.

Stalking on carefully he thought of the eagle, of the day. He was cautious but the more outlandish and alien the terrain became, the more at ease Stig seemed to be.

Up from the slow density pushed a string of grey smoke to break the subdued white sky, uniform and weatherless. Mick stopped and looked at the smoke for a second.

—No smoke without fire and no fire without life . . . but what?

His heart started to gain pace and adrenaline. His mouth parched almost immediately and he dragged his warm breath across his tongue. He thought of the small men who had so suddenly brought death to the deer. He thought of what they might do to him and Stig. His thoughts were in vain. Stig had bolted into the clearing wagging and smiling in the green oasis. The dog was greeted at the fire by a dark hand holding and offering a lump of white meat. He accepted the meat easily and held it steady between two front paws as he licked and tore at it.

Mick crept closer knowing that the small people knew he was there. They had followed him all day. They knew where he had slept and for how long. They knew how uneasily he had crept through the woods. They even knew how he felt in the pit of his stomach. But still they remained seated around the fire drinking and murmuring low.

They drank from clay pots. Near the fire Mick could make out a shack of sorts, made up haphazard from logs and sticks and twigs and mud. Most were made from silver birch and hid in a silver birch thicket so that it faded into the background when you looked away. Branches were entwirled and encurled through the walls of the shack to help bind them together. Mud had been thrown on to make the construction wind and rainproof. It stood there like some hideous form of tree.

By now, unawares, Mick had edged out from his sparse cover into full view of the little men by the fire. They remained seated. Some were raking about in the embers with sticks. Mick stood rigid staring eye to eye with one. There was no malice in the man's eyes. The fear in Mick was quashed, he felt at ease. All seemed mystifying yet homely. He was only slightly disturbed when he stepped forwards at the old man's signal. A slow beckoning movement of the arm like a priest to a young boy. Mick sat on the edge of the log shifting his eyes left to right then flitting them all around him. He was still afraid to look at the men yet compelled to be there, right there sitting on that log. He let an unsure smile flicker before turning to the hypnotic colours of the fire. He let his mind sink into the flames, into a world of fiery shadows and embers that glowed like life itself in the roots of the flames. The fire glowed and sank to glow again. It lit up faces then hid them.

Mick had his clasped hands gently prised open by a big grubby, dark pair of hands. The nails were like toenails. A clay pot was thrust into his hands and raised to his lips. He was motioned to drink. Other eyes were wide and smiling, nodding and urging him. They repeatedly jerked their own pots to their lips and removed them so that he would understand. He looked into the pot at the opaque liquid. He swallowed. He lifted the pot to his lips letting

43

the contents pass into an apprehensive mouth.

He never expected it to taste so good. It was like drinking love, love that melted the soul. The magic ran through his body like fire, like a forest fire on a July heatwave. His brain rested easy in his head and his eyes felt sleepy.

The fire had come to life again with a ferocity that bit into the sky then threw itself against the wind to shine and crawl on the whiteness of the dog snurled up like a shellfish on a rock. Stig lay beside the fire asleep, digesting the meal. He looked all sorts of odd shapes and sizes as the light turned his whites into red and the blacks into non-existence. Mick smiled as he handed the jug back to the old man with the shining eyes. He had never felt so drawn into something as he was into these eyes.

The old man, whose face was sixty and lay like leather on his head, had the athletic body of a thirty-year-old, refilled Mick's jug. He drank greedily at the brew spilling it down both cheeks. The men laughed low. He jolted at the fire of the drink, removed it from his lips and returned it. The old man handed Mick a metal disc.

The man's deep eyes smiled. Mick smiled back. The drink had got into him now. For a moment he thought of a thing; a thing so unreal it shocked him. Then it was gone and he was powerless to bring it back.

He woke early next morning on a wooden bench near the loch. He stared at the sky briefly and wondered where he was. He swung around on the seat and sat folded over and cold, put his head in his hands to position his eyes on the soothing water. It lay flat in the peaceful morning like a slither of white plastic. The swans skimmed along the surface like they were flat bottomed and driven by an unseen force. He spotted Stig as the dog tried to sneak up on crows that had landed near some bread.

Four fishermen sat on the banks. As Mick stood up something fell to the ground and stuck into the peaty soil. He looked down. It was a disc. He cleaned it on his trousers and held it up searching its contours and shape curiously. A small, bronze disc a little bigger than a ten-pence. As the dirt came off he noticed the markings – they looked like mountains.

At this he remembered the woods and the deer, the killing and the small dark men. He thought of the old man who had given him the drink and the drink. He remembered all this in the quick succession of someone who wakes with a hangover and pieces together the night before.

So all the small details came back and wrapped themselves around the first thoughts of the day. Time had gone like a fluff-clock in the wind. He had no hangover. He felt a distance from the world, a step back from it, alien.

He felt relaxed walking through the grass watching the dog at play. He paused and thought of the dark men and then walked on. He reached into his pocket and took out the disc. Stared. He turned a full circle looking for a clue as to where he might have been, where he might have got lost. There were no clues. When he left the countryside, for the anonymity of the town, the dark people turned back and headed to their place beneath the rushing winds.

Is that your car, Sir?

When I stayed down in the south side of the Brig I had this neighbour. A right sleazy bastard. Oh! I hated him but he hated me even more. He used to phone the Polis an the Housin an what not. Ye couldn't move for him peepin out the curtain an whisperin about how I was drunk an smashed the house up or this that an the next thing. He was one of them wee fat bastards that looked like he sprayed his body wi chip-fat every mornin. His hair was black an welded to his head. His wife was the exact same only wi tits an a fanny. Christ ye should get put in jail for lettin the likes o that breed. Bit they bred all right. Oh ay.

Skweek skweek skweek

their bed would go every night. She'd howl like a laughin

faced hyena an he'd grunt an flap onto her like a walrus. Made me puke so it did. An Carmen'd not go near me then cos it made her sick an all. So ye can imagine it. He's gettin his hole every night an all I can do is wrestle wi it like it's a crocodile or somethin. Know what I mean? Choke the bishop . . . German tank.

I was prayin for an excuse to kick his cunt in. Any excuse. I mean I'm not a violent guy but know how sometimes ye've got to teach them a lesson? Well he needed teachin.

Right ye got the picture now? So wait t'ye hear this. Carmen goes to the van this night . . . —two bottles Irn Bru, two Marathons, forty Club king size, a double nougat, a Curly Wurly an whatever ye want for yourself, I shouts out the windy. She nods all the way to the van without lookin up. I mind her arms were folded an she had this white woollen dress on. It was glowin in the yella streetlights. Man it stuck to her skin. Ye could see every groove. I decided I was goin to shag her that night so I shoves a porno in the video so as to warm her up.

I flops back on the couch an sparks up the half a joint I've got lyin there. I don't want ye to think I'm a slob nor nothin. At that time I was at the weights an I was jaggin masel up wi Deca Durabolin an Testosterone. I was solid. Fifteen an a half stone. But I like to relax at night wi a couple a joints, a few cans an a bottle a Buckie.

So there's me lying on the couch. Restin from a chest shoulders an arms night at the gym. I'm well stoned. I starts to notice a long time passes cos the porno is nearly finished an no Carmen. I rolls off the couch an looks out the windy. Nothin. Only the young team tooled up wi baseball bats an stuff gettin it thegether to mangle the Mad Squad.

But where the fuck is she?

says I. I was a bit jealous then so ma brain's doin overtime. The young team waves up an I wave back.

—YO! I shouts.

—Mick ma man! they shout back.

All this time I'm noticin this pump up yer trainers music. I'm not daft so it's not long before I realises there's a party in Greasy Bastards. I know what yer thinkin . . . but that's where she was.

Fuck me . . .

she goes to the van an on the way back as nice as ye like, halfway up the close she disappears into his house. I went fuckin mental.

I only knew she was in there cos Aul Nosy Bastard down the stairs phoned me up. —Oh by the way, she goes, —Carmen's in the party next door.

—Carmen's in the fuckin what, I goes. —What the fuck's goin on?

Carmen never spoke to the bastards in her life. She goes to the van an there she is dancin wi some stranger at this party. Nosy Aul Bastard down the stair isn't content wi that. No way. She starts sayin stuff like, —I'll tell ye this there's no way I'm goin to a party wi the like o hur again . . . she's a hussy . . . I'm tellin ye yer burd's a scrubber. I'm callin Aul Bastard all the whores under the sun an shoutin, —don't you talk about ma burd like that. But on an on she goes all about how she left cos Carmen's in the room wi this bird's man . . .

BLACKOUT
RAGE

. . . an there's the phone swingin on its wire.

I'm bangin at the fuckin door. Ye could fry eggs on me. I'm hot as fuck. Electric. There's scurryin an tooin an froin then Greasy Bastard opens the door. He's sweatin an right there I think he's been shaggin ma burd. But then Carmen comes sideways out a room an so does this guy. A right flashy good-lookin bastard. The kind ye keep well away from yer burd. Well I'm goin mental an Carmen worms her way out an stands behind me. I can still smell the sweat an perfume. I can still see a string of hair stickin to her neck. Flashy bastard goes for this big fancy vase an swings it right it me. But he's dealin wi the maddest bastard in the Brig so does I not just fuck the head right on the vase as it's comin at me an it splinters into a million bits. The blood's runnin out ma head an he's shitin hisself. He can't move. I crashed the head on him an cos he's already agin a wall he's out like a light. I put the boot in a couple a times so he gets the message. Turns out he's a commando type in the army.

Special Forces? —Some fuckin army,
says I.

Greasy Bastard whips out this big blunt bread knife an lunges. I've still got the scar. I grabs it by the blade an laughs like Jack Nicholson. He shat hissel. I grabs his hair wi ma left hand an swings him round into the close. I mind the first punch. It was a cross between a right hook an a straight right. I got the full fifteen stone behind it an

whack.

But he ducked a bit. I was trying to break his nose but I scudded the forehead. Man his head burst like a kipper an down he went. I took the boot off his ribs a couple a times an left him wrigglin on the close floor an went in an waited for the Polis. Carmen went to bed wi her clothes on so as I couldn't see the love bites an her ripped knickers. She loved gettin her underwear ripped. That turned her right on. I was the man for them games . . . rough stuff. I knew the score wi her. She was hidin.

The Polis never came.

The next time I sees Greasy Bastard I'm up at the Paki's gettin a couple a Supers to take the drooth away an when I comes into the close he's on his hands an knees wipin the blood off the floor.

—Good Morning, I goes an he's said it back before he realises it's me. He's got a load a stitches across his head. He puts his head down an scrubs frantic like he can't get this bit off. I goes in the house an bursts out laughin. He probably never got the Polis cos he tried to rip me wi thon knife an then there's action man wi the big fancy vase an all that. He'd not want the Army to know that some ordinary guy welded him. I mean, how'ye supposed to save the fuckin country wi that talent? Special fuckin Operations? He'll be needin special operations if he goes near ma burd again.

The next week Greasy Bastard sent a hunner people to ma door.

The Priest came an asked if we wanted to get married.

The Housin came an told us to stop annoying the neighbours.

The Polis came this night when I was watchin Flight Of The Condor. They told me to stop the wild party an then asked to see Carmen. Someday had phoned up an said I was doin her in. Wonder who the fuck that was? She was sleepin.

The Social came. I was in the lobby cupboard. Carmen was on a Monday Book an I was gettin the Giro sent to ma

Maw's. They looked in all the wardrobes. Carmen says the clothes were mine but I'm in London in jail or somethin.

A Jehovah's Witni came.

—Fuck off were Catholics, says Carmen.

Off goes the Witni all humble like an up come the Mormons.

Slam. Off ye pop Mormons. Good night.

An then we're out for a drink this night an the Polis break in. Greasy Bastard tells them we left the washin machine on an flooded the close. I might have left it on. If we fuckin had one. I goes bananas wi the Polis, fuck youse an all this. I'm goin ten to the dozen jumpin about like a madman. They never even apologised. They were goin to lift me. Carmen's holdin the arms behind ma back an they're tryin to get me to hit them. The neighbours are all out to see what the fuck's goin on. The only one that's not out is Greasy Welded Hair an that's how I know it's him. As if I needed proof.

I decided to get the fuckin bastard for once an for all.

The next week he putters in the street wi a beat-up aul Metro. Make ye sick – they're all out there Mammy Grease, Daddy Grease an assorted Granny an Granda Greasies an some wee Greasies. They're inspectin this car like they know about motors. Christ, I don't know much about motors but from behind the curtain I could see it was a fuckin rust bucket. An what's he doin but smilin up at me as if to say, *Well Hard Man what do ye think of ma new car then? Us Greasies are really comin up in the world now eh!* Oh! I could've punched lumps out him but he's still wearin the bandage an that's a liberty, so I decides to get him in some pub or somethin. Kick fuck right out him – hospital case.

The next mornin do I not see the openin I've been lookin for? There's this horn beep beepin so I looks out the windy along wi a million other fuckers. It's not for me. It's drivin lessons. I wait at the windy in case it's that seventeen-year aul honey in the cottage types. An who comes bobbin out the close like he's goin to collect the European Cup? Right – Greasy Bastard. Off he pops for drivin lesson number one. Right there Nosy Bastard phones up an goes, Ain't that terrible him drivin about in a wee car an he's got no licence an no insurance nor nothin. By the way I'm still no talkin to Carmen so a hands her the phone without sayin nothin. Nosy aul bastard fills her in on what's what.

Later on when Grease is back an

skweek skweekin

away there like drivin must turn him on. Or she's turned on cos he's a real man now wi a car an all that shite. She starts her laughin faced hyena stuff an I picks up the phone an phones the Polis. He falls on her gruntin an I'm thinkin it might be the same bed Carmen got her special operation on.

—Hello Coatbridge Police, can I help you, goes this posh voice.

I tells them how there's this maniac in the street who's got a car – it might be stolen – I goes. I tells them he's screechin into the street like Mad Max an he'll kill a wean soon. The rust bucket wouldn't go over twenty but I lays it on thick so they'll come an get the bastard. An him just gave his wife one. Sittin there sharin sweat soaked roll-ups an restin their bellies on their thighs.

The Polis come into the street an they're lookin round the cars. Yes, I says. Fuckin yes!! I can't wait to see his face. —Fuck you an yer smelly wee Metro, I shouts.

—Come on see this, I tells Carmen an fills her in on what the score is. She loves it an takes the scullery windy. I takes the livin room. The Polis look up at the close an look in their wee books. Up they come. Windows are twitchin everywhere. Me an Carmen run to the door an press the aul ears on it. Probably that's what Greasy Bastard was doin too.

BANG

BANG

BANG

goes ma door. Me an Carmen jump up. We looks at each other.

BANG

BANG

BANG

goes the door again. Carmen crawls in the toilet. She swings the door shut. I opens the door an there's two big Polis an they're the ones I was goin to do in the week before.

—Are you Mr Riley?

—Ay?

—Is that your car, Sir?

—No, the wee Metro? *IT BELONGS TO MA NEIGHBOURS,* I shouts.

—No . . . not the Austin Metro, Mr Riley, the Renault Five.

Well fuck sake – shut ma fuckin mouth . . . do they not go an do me for no tax on the Renault Five an Greasy Bastard gets off Scot free wi the whole thing? Taught me a lesson that. I'll stick to dishin out doins in the future.

Big Beefie

I had to stop sharp turnin the corner. The brakes screeched an this big guy turned, stooped an zoomed his head into the windscreen. Maura cringed, her nails dug into the seats. I had seen the iron bar in his right hand but she only noticed it when it clanged off the bonnet.

—Oh my God . . . look . . . he's got a metal thing.

She looks at me wonderin why I wasn't panickin.

—It's only Big Beefie.

Big Beefie leaned further into the dim light of the car. Some more cars piled up behind his traffic jam. His face was framed by a great twist of metal.

—Oh my God, what's that stuff all over his face? she screams.

Beefie's jaw was held together by metal scaffoldin. He looked like Hannibal the Cannibal. Maura breathed rapidly an ripped the seat, breakin her newly manicured nails.

—Drive back . . . drive back . . . She screams twistin away from the evil grin and smoky breath on the glass.

He raised the bar into the night focusin on ma face. Two morons high on jellies shuffled to the side window grinnin. The drunk corner boys chanted:

BEE—FIE! BEE—FIE!

BEE—FIE! BEE—FIE!

BEE—FIE! BEE—FIE!

BEE—FIE! BEE—FIE!

His scaffoldin clicked against the glass. I could see the silver mesh an he could see me clearly for the first time. His sidekicks were bouncin the car to an fro to the chants of the corner boys. Beefie would have to do somethin now.

But he didn't.

He shouted somethin sharp an withdrew rapidly. His puzzled sidekicks scuttled away. Beefie gaped an nodded holdin a palm to the inside of the car an backed off.

—What's he doing now? What's he doing now?

—S'alright, s'alright. He's changed his mind.

I drove on. I gave Beefie The Stare. The corner boys stopped singin an for a moment Mitchell Street seemed normal. We passed under the railway bridge an stopped at the Mill Brae lights. Ye could hear sirens in the distance.

—Looks like Beefie found a head for his iron bar, I says to Maura all casual like.

—My God . . . do you think those cars are for him!!?

Three police cars sped downhill blastin. An ambulance. The lights changed an we drove away slowly lookin downhill all the while.

—Do you really think that he's hit some poor soul with that metal thing?

—Probably.

—He was crazy looking. She paused an then asked, all puzzled, —Why do you think he never touched us?

—Did ye see the metal on his face?

—Yes. All that stuff. What was that? An American footballer mask?

—Naw, it's a broken jaw. His mouth's gettin held thegether so it can heal up.

—He's got a broken jaw and he's out drinking? She was amazed.

—Hmm . . . it would only surprise me if Beefie was sober!

—Do you think that he's out looking for the people who did that to him?

—Oh . . . Ay . . . I think he's out to get someone for it alright . . . anyone.

She didn't understand.

—What do you mean?

—Well . . . remember our David got mugged a couple a weeks ago? An they took his Reggae Blaster an hunner quid leather jacket?

She remembered. She nodded rapidly wi her mouth shut tight.

—Well it was Big Beefie an his crew that done it.

She couldn't make sense of what I was sayin. I helped her.

—Ah smashed his jaw . . . got im up Wine Alley an kicked fuck out him . . . an ah'll tell ye somethin . . . got the stuff back first thing next mornin.

She never spoke all the way to her house.

Peck on the cheek.

—I'll phone, she says an walks quickly away.

Kitbags an Tiny Tears

It was the sixties. In them days the Das had to steal; coal one night, spuds the next an back to coal the next. Yer time was taken up wi gettin a fire up an gettin chips to go wi the bread an tubs of axle-grease. (That's what he called margarine). There was about five or six of us then an more on the way. The houses in Kirkwood were damp an fallin down discarded mine-shafts.

I can mind ma Maw singin in the livin room. Now an then she'd press her cheek against the window to see if ma Da was comin up the street wi the dog an an Army kitbag full of coal or spuds. He went wi Mr Harnes cos they had a lot of weans too. I mind ma Maw's eyes sparkin in the black window panes like the only stars in the sky. She'd sing:

Oh Mary this London's a wonderful sight
where the people are workin by day an by night . . .

Caroline used to sing it to her doll tryin to copy the words
as they come out ma Maw's mouth. It was a Tiny-Tears. If
ye were a girl an ye wanted a doll, that was the one that ye
wanted. The thing about Tiny-Tears; she cried real tears. I
mind when the light was cut off an the candle's flame looked
like it was burnin in the tear. Weird! The white skin looked
like a dead baby's. It frightened me but I never let on. Once
I seen it crawlin over the floor on its own but when I told
ma Maw I got slapped an got ten Hail Marys off of Father
Davanny.

Ma Maw stopped singin an her wave squeaked off the
chilly glass. The deep, woof-woofs of Kim came driftin up
the darkness. I pulled myself up so ma eyes were over the
window ledge. Ma Maw must've been a slip of a lass then.
Madly in love intent only on feedin the weans an heatin the
house.

The front door creaked an the night sliced the rooms.
We had no carpets in them days. Ma Da rushed through
like a cold whirlwind an out the back door. Usual. There
was the whine of metal then the low rumble of coal pourin
into a bunker. Mrs Adams came in the front door cuddlin a
big parcel of butcher meat tied up wi string. The blood off
the meat was seepin through the brown paper. Kim was
right in there rippin at the paper. I was the only one that
noticed.

—Jack Frost's out an about the night, youse weans
better git yer banes up tae the fire til yer Maw makes yer
supper.

Another rumble. Mrs Adam's (whose man was dead)
coal-bunker was gettin coal too. That's why ma Da took so

long to come home this night; cos he had two bags of the coal. That's how she gave us the butcher-meat. She knew the butcher right well. She handed the parcel to ma Maw. Kim snapped up the bits of meat before they hit the floor.

GULP! GULP! GULP! GULP!

. . .all the way to the scullery.

Ma Da came back to the front door all red an shiny an breathin vapour out his nose like a bull. He smiled an rubbed his hands like a little boy.

Mrs Adams told him thanks Pat an pushed by Mr Harnes's arse as he bent over the railins smokin. In a big voice like a paper seller Harnes shouts,

Raw . . . nnaay . . . Jay . . . may.

Ronnie an Jamie appeared out the blackness. They swifted away a kitbag each without words.

—Tell yer Maw there's a delivery the morra night, he says in a whisper that would grate cheese. The hairs on ma neck went mad. We all knew what that meant. The coal came from the brickwork. Ye had to cross The Viaduct an climb a steep embankment to get to it. Sometimes a train would come when they were halfway across an they'd have to lean out into the hundred-foot drop counter-balanced by the kitbag of coal.

Ye had to be careful not to take too much coal an ruin

a good thing. But on a delivery night ye could take tons. On these nights the atmosphere in the street was like a carnival. All the Das an Maws went down an up all night humphin coal till every bunker was full to the gunwales. Any wummin that never had a man or a big son got her bunker filled an she'd watch for the Polis or make tea an that. We all brightened up wi the thought of a delivery.

There was a watchie on the place but he never said nothin since the night he came out to ma Da . . .

—Right what's goin on here, he shouted stampin down through the dross dust at ma Da an Mr Harnes. (I heard ma Da tellin this story when he was drunk at New Year.) Kim said *Woof Woof* an the Watchie stopped an shouted, —This is private property.

—Get yerself to fuck. We're takin this tae warm the weans.

The words don't sound much but it's the way he said them. The Watchie, took one short look, an went back to the hut. He never comes out now especially on a delivery night when ye can't tell the coal from the people all black an movin. It's funny right enough . . . over the years the wummin in the street had taken to send him Christmas cards an bits of bakin an stuff.

—He's jist a poor aul sowl fae Bargeddie . . . no different tae us, I heard Mrs Harnes say one day when Mr Harnes was talkin about him. Crazy thing was . . . Mr Harnes worked in the Brickwork durin the day.

Caroline was busy tellin her doll that tomorrow was a delivery night and it'd need to be in bed early an all this dolly talk rubbish, when we were bundled off to bed. She bunged Tiny-Tears into the Silver Cross pram after kissin its plastic nose. Four or five piled in one bed an all the coats were flung on. I got ma two feet in a sleeve, leaned down, folded the end, an conked out.

The next day had white frosted ferns patterned on the window. I reached up an rubbed a hole wi ma toe. I kept ma leg in the sleeve. But I was warm cos today was delivery day an already the street was squeakin wi people up an down collectin bogeys an prams an anythin that went on wheels. The women could shove these while the men carry the kitbags. Up an down they'd go from first dark to first light.

The night was a long time before it came. A silent gang assembled at the end of the street an a fog of breath hovered. There was a buzz suddenly rose when the last orange flakes of sun fell from the bare trees an a magnification of squeakin as off they went towards the delivery. A muffled cheer went up from the wummin. All through the night them that never went came in an out of the houses makin tea an boilin spuds an givin out pokes of chips.

—Are youse weans alright?

—Ay! we'd shout back no matter what we were up to.

We'd huddle on the stairs till we were freezin an then scoot back in for a roastin at the fire. It was better than Christmas. Our squeaky voices sang wi pram wheels. The Das' an Big Sons' voices droned out of movin black shapes lit by wet stars in a slippy sky. Ye could tell who was comin up the street by the drone. Ye never heard what they said but ye could tell who it was. We used to guess an ye got givin everybody a good punch or a dead-leg if ye were right an they were wrong. It went the way it always went that night. I woke up bein carried to bed an ma Da whisperin to ma Maw about how this time the coal would last for months.

I used to wonder what the coalman thought when he came round an nobody wanted any.

•

Waaaaaaaaaaaaaaaaaaaaaaaaaaaaaa

I woke up the next day to Caroline roarin her eyes out an all the cupboards an bags tumbled out all over the floor. Ma Maw came stampin into the room an grabbed her shoulders.

—Wheesht . . . wheeesht . . . yer Da's sleepin through the wall . . . he's been out at work all night . . . do ye want to waken him?

That's when I found out Caroline wasn't as scared of ma Da as the rest of us, cos she paused an went,

Waaaaaaaaaaaaaaaaaaaaaaaaaaaaaa

Ma Maw covered over her mouth. We giggled from the warmth of the bed. Ye couldn't see through the window for the ferns but ye could see how white it was outside cos the room was lit up like summer. Ma Maw took her hand away slowly.

—Now I can't help ye if ye don't tell me what it is?

—Ma . . . ma . . . ma . . . Tiny-Tears . . . she's away . . . she's ran away in the middle of the night . . . she's not nowhere an I can't find her an an . . .

Waaaaaaaaaaaaaaaaaaaaaaaaaaaaaa

She wails again like she could swallow the moon. Ma Da coughs an we all go rigid. Even Caroline lowers the wailin.

Waaaaaaaaaaaaaaaaaaaaaaaaaaaaaaaaa, she goes

—Don't be silly now . . . goes ma Maw – I can hear laughing in her voice.

—Dolls can't just get up an dance a jig right out of the house anytime they want to.

—I saw it crawlin along the floor last week. I knew I shouldn't've said that. I could hear muffled slaps. I murmured awches from under the blankets.

—Just-you-keep-out-of-this, says ma Maw hittin the blankets. She hit everyone but me an they all started roarin an stickin their heads out coats an blankets for attention. It was like a cartoon. Caroline *Waaaaa'd* even louder cos it was her thunder they were stealin; her time to cry. I burrowed into the world of coats an jackets where ye might never be found. The door swings open an ma Da coughs.

Silence.

—Whit's goin on here Alice? he shouts. He sounds angry. He sounds tired. Caroline sobs hopin that he's goin to get lookin for Tiny-Tears but I knew all he wanted was peace an quiet. I never needed ma head above the blankets for that.

—She's lost her Tiny-Tears, says ma Maw in a voice so gentle that I nearly came out of the coats to see who was talkin.

—She whit?

—She's lost her Tiny-Tears doll. She put it in the pram an now it's gone.

—It wasn't in the pram last night . . . mind? We ditched the fuckin thing when the axle broke.

Ma Maw stares into his face like she was watchin a film an then nods.

—That's right . . . that's right. I would've seen it if was there.

Waaaaaaaaaaaaaaaaaaaaaaaaaaaaaa

said Caroline, realisin the doll was gone forever.

The door went an it was Betty Harnes. They gave her the whole story about the missin Tiny Tears while she puffed Woodbine after Woodbine.

Then, somethin strange happened. Her face straightened out. It was wrinkly as a plate of porridge most of the time an her eyes used to hide behind bags an layers of skin. For a second it went flat an smooth an I could see a girl. She looked at Caroline wi that shinin face.

—D'ye believe in majuck hen? she asked. She talked funny cos she was a gypsy.

—Whit . . . whit kinda magic? sobs Caroline.

It was the first I knew about White witches an Black witches an Banshees an all horrible things that ye never talked about. They eventually agreed that Caroline believed in White witches cos they weren't so scary as the other things. Betty Harnes got Caroline to do this wee dance on one leg, hoppin about in a circle. She'd to stick a finger in her ear an keep her eyes shut an sing this wee song three times to the powers of the White witch. It was a song about the Black witch;

> Nowhere I do declare
> her equal ye could find.
> She was humphy-backit an pock-markit
> an one of her eyes was blind.
> She'd feet for killin clocks wi
> an bunions on her toes.
> She be a regular Dandy
> if she had a shorter nose.

Caroline opened her eyes. The raven eyes of Betty Harnes

shut them again. She sang on, spinnin round the room on one leg. I was watchin by now out of a coat sleeve that smelt of old women an mothballs.

> *Nowhere I do declare*
> *her equal ye could find.*
> *She was humphy-backit an pock-markit*
> *an one of her eyes was blind.*
> *She'd feet for killin clocks wi*
> *an bunions on her toes.*
> *She be a regular Dandy*
> *if she had a shorter nose.*

On she went without hardly waitin for breath. When Caroline came round an opened her eyes an steadied herself from the dizziness an when the room steadied she saw Betty Harnes was gone.

Waaaaaaaaaaaaaaaaaaaaaaaaaaaaaa

she screamed again. By this time we were rubbin holes in the frost followin Betty Harnes up the street. She went to the phone box.

—It's OK Caroline . . . says ma Maw . . . She's away up the phone box to phone the White Witch an tell her about Tiny-Tears.

I remember bein amazed at witches wi phones. Caroline wiped her snotters on her cuff an climbed onto the bed. She wiped the steam of our breaths off one of the holes an caught Betty Harnes goin in the box an messin about. Ye could see she was stuffin money in an Caroline seemed happy from then until Mr Harnes came to our door on his way home from work. He usually talks to ma Da quiet in the scullery. That's why I was extra surprised when he asked to see Caroline. We all followed her into the scullery where he sat wi both arms folded on his work-bag on the table.

—Well, weans.

He had a crazy stare, a big sailor beard an he looked like a madman. We stared.

—there I was a donnerin hame frae ma work like I've done a million times . . . a million times. I'm lookin forward to gettin a bit scran intae ma belly an a sit down an a good smoke at the fire. It's jist like any ither night, min, an I comes up the lane at Mitchell Street there. It's black, as black as a night can be an a shiver runs down ma aul spine of a sudden. I stops . . . ye know the way when ye jist know there's somethin watchin yer every move?

We all nods an huddle thegether. Ma Maw an Da are noddin wildly too. He gives us a good starin each an goes on.

—I'm right there in the middle o the lane an I hears this voice. I stops dead an in the panic. I don't know to run back or run furrit. I freeze . . . then . . . I hears the voice again. It's right low an squeaky.

—Help me . . . help me . . . it shouts. I looks round but can't see a livin soul. I listens but there's nothin. Like there's nobody alive in the whole town.

—Help me . . .help me, it goes again. It sounds like a wean in trouble so I whispers, where are ye . . .? I can't see ye . . .

—I'm in here . . . is that you Mr Harnes?

Well . . . Jesus Mary an Joseph the fright it gave me knowin ma name an all. I thought I'd been sent for an was about to start prayin when it goes,

—I'm in here . . . in the pram . . .

In the darkness I never noticed the pram lyin on its side so I strikes a match an leans down to the gunwales of the pram but there's nothin in it. Just a big empty space.

His eyes bulge at us. We're as quiet as the insides of the coal-bunkers.

—I was terrified by then an about to run when out of the empty pram the voice comes again, this time it's cryin,

—Oh Mr Harnes please . . . please don't go away an leave me . . . I'm in the bottom of the pram . . . in the secret bit . . . It's Tiny-Tears and I belong to Caroline Riley twenty-four Drumpark Street . . . please take me home. It's so cold in this pram and if I stay out another night Jack Frost will get me an I'll die.

Well . . . My GOD!! Help! Help! I shouted an ripped open the secret bit an there she was . . . cryin real tears . . . an a wet nappy too . . .

As he was talkin Mr Harnes dragged the doll out his bag.

BABY BABY BABY BABY BABY

BABY BABY BABY BABY BABY

screams Caroline grabbin it shoutin an runnin away to the fire squeezin the life out of it. Ma Maw an Da laughed wi Mr Harnes an the rest of us stared about the steamy room in puzzled amazement.

Crilley

—Whit d'ye make of Johnny's wee pal?

I looks at her. Obviously a story I haven't heard.

—Whit d'ye mean . . . is that another one of the young team chibbed or somethin?

—Did ye not know about it . . .?

Guess number one wrong.

Ma Da buts in from cookin somethin messy in a pot.

—It's a fuckin shame that so it is . . . that laddie Crilley . . . an there was Mrs McCusker, just the other day, out there knockin lumps out Mrs Crilley because of that sign on her fence. I'm none the wiser still.

—Crilley . . . the IRA guy, ma Maw says so I can pinpoint him.

—IRA ma fuckin arse, ma Da corrects, still stirrin.

Ma Maw draws him a stop-that-swearin look. They both look at me waitin for recognition. An image of the toothless Crilley drunk an on the beg forms.

—Crilley? I say noddin ma head an pointin to the newly roughcasted house across the street. I pause a bit.

—Crilley . . . him that me an Tam roughcasted the house . . . lime green for fucksake?

—Ay that's him. Remember his mother put the poster up on her back fence?

We all laugh. Mrs Crilley drank three litre bottles of LD a day. One day, full of it, she puts this sign up on her back fence.

Mrs Mcusker owes me £25 and wont pay she is a skinflint

I remember that alright. Mrs McCusker never ripped it down. People came from all over to read the notice like it was a proclamation.

We stops laughin.

Silence.

—So what about him anyway? Is he dead or somethin?

—Just as good is, says ma Da.

Ma Maw blesses his poor wee soul a couple of times.

—Have ye started goin to the aul chapel mammy dear?

—She was there last week an now she's a holy roller. Jesus this that an the next thing. If it moves she blesses it. If it stands still she blesses it an if it makes a noise she chucks holy water all over it. Ma Da shakes his head an stirs the pot.

—He took an overdose. A vegetable, goes ma Maw. More silence.

—An overdose? On purpose?

—Ay, he tried to get his Mother's sleepin pills so as to sell them for more drink but she wanted to sell them for more drink herself. So he begged her an promised he'd bring her half the drink back. She was goin to do that, when the Da comes in an wants more drink so they all fight an argue about who gets the pills. The Da attacks Crilley but this time Crilley does him in, rips the tablets from the Mother's hands an bolts. By this time it's two in the mornin an all he's got is the dregs in a bottle a Buckfast. He couldn't face the night without drink so he swallows all the tablets. But it was ten times too much, him that skinny an all. Wee Polecat the milkboy found him at six in the mornin – he's supposed to be brain dead.

—Polecat? I goes. —I know that.

Nobody laughed. I sigh an lean over to see if I can get a sense of blackness from Crilley's house. The lime green roughcast seems absurd in the rainy day. The windows are dark an net curtains hang down like they've given up. The overgrown back garden is bein blown about an two barkin lurchers spin around each other markin off tussocks an old pishy mattresses. It's clear that I'm not goin to say anythin so ma Da does.

—Our Johnny won't even go up an visit him . . . his best pal! Whit are they like? In ma day . . . An off he goes Blah Blah Blah.

—Probably can't bring hissel to see him there, all the tubes an that comin out him, says Maw. A flickerin of images rips through ma brain.

—Every time I come over here somebody's been murdered or put in a coma or done theirself in or done somebody else in.

—Ay. It's a sad place right enough. We can only pray for them.

She hands me a coffee an sits down. Ma Da stirs the pot an we don't say nothin. Outside the rain's rattlin off the rose bushes knockin petals to the ground.

—It's a wonder she's out an about drinkin anyway, says ma Maw.

—Who?

—Mrs Crilley . . . since she stabbed her man.

It's comin back to me. All the things that went wrong for the Crilleys.

—Ay. Ma Maw goes on. —Full of wine . . . she waited till he was sleepin. Rumour has it that he was nippin her from over the flats that goes to the dancin wi the teenagers. Who would want a fat pig like him but? Anyway, thirty six times she stuck it intae him . . . an he lived. He was out the hospital in two weeks tellin his story for drink up The Hotel an down in The Woodside. Right enough he was a right bad arse in his day him. I went to his door the day to tell him we were gettin a mass said for his son . . .

—Telt ye she's a holy roller.

She looks at ma Da. They smile an she carries on.

—I chaps the door . . .

73

—Nothin.

—I hears shoutin an that so I chaps it again, light.

—Silence.

—Ye know that silence that ye know somebody's listenin. Well suddenly the door swings open. The creepy bastard must've snuck along the lobby. I smiles at him but he just glares an sticks his chest out.

—An who are you may I ask? he says in a posh voice.

—It's Mrs Riley from across the lane . . . your son . . . Crilley, we're goin to get a mass said.

—Well! his expression changes an it's all —Oh hello Sadie . . . oh it's a sad thing . . . I know . . . thanks for your concern.

—But all the time from the back room I hears, Who the fucks that . . .? who the fuck is it . . .? tell them to fuck aff an git in here ya bastard . . . git me a drink, d'ye hear me?!!! D'ye fuckin hear me?

—I ignore it an he says —Well I'll tell her when she comes in . . . thanks. We'll probably visit him tomorrow.

—He closes the door slowly peekin out an leaves me standin in the rain.

—Their son's lyin there in a coma an they'll *PROBABLY VISIT HIM TOMORROW*, I shouts.

—No wonder he tried to do hisself in, says ma Da tastin the stuff in the pot. —Whit, wi all that an a lime green house – done up like a Blackpool bedsit for fucksake.

—It was an accident, says Maw tryin to defend him.

I looks up the lane an here's our Johnny bobbin down like it's just another ordinary day. I keep an intense eye on him an notice his eyes swivel as he passes the Crilley's back gate.

Mrs Mcusker owes me £25 and wont pay she is a skinflint

His head doesn't move. I can tell he's drunk before he comes in. I can always tell that. He walks like he's confident. The door chaps an ma Maw says,

—That'll be our Johnny, Pat, better let him in. Ma Da coughs an walks out the scullery.

—Our poor wee Johnny. He must be worried about Crilley, she says to me in the voice she uses for babies an animals.

Johnny comes in an we all ignore the stench of Buckfast.

—Awright, he says noddin an pushin by me to get to the sink. I know he's thinkin a drink of water'll take away the smell.

—Whit's this about wee Crilley then?

Johnny decides on the tough approach.

—Oh Crilley . . . Some burd ditched him an he tanned his Maw's tablets.

—I thought it was cos of his Mother, Johnny? asks ma Maw.

—Ye never git the right story down here . . . ye should know that by now, says ma Da.

Johnny drags out a chair. —Fag! he demands an ma

Maw chucks him one out her packet. He sparks it up. We're all waitin as he sucks in a good long draw like he's seen on the telly. I alternate ma looks between the Crilley's house an him. Ma Da watches the stuff an Johnny an ma Maw watches us all. Nothin was stirrin in the Crilley's. Ma Maw sits an ashtray down beside Johnny an he blows a long line of smoke. He pouts a couple of smoke rings for ma attention an starts.

—He was in The Woodside on Friday . . .

—That's his giro day, ma Maw tells me, noddin. Johnny sighs at bein interrupted. Ma Da stops stirrin.

—He was in The Woodside wi Milky Bar an Polecat an there was nothin wrong. He was cool . . . loaded wi dough . . . half a Q . . . good few jugs. Usual.

His vowels got longer as he told the story an he was talkin out the side of his mouth. Ma Da notices this too an gives me the nod sayin nothin.

—We're all sittin there an his burd comes in. They never even fought. She usually goes ape-shit an drags him out the pub. Member she tumlered him last year?

We all nod. Crilley got twenty-odd stitches that time.

—This time she's OK. Jist in for the money an her cargo an a bit off the half Q.

—What's a half kew? asks ma Maw. Ma Da's all ears.

—A half quarter a dope . . . he says as if he's their Da.

—Aw ay, whacky baccy, says ma Maw. Ma Da resumes his stirrin.

Says Johnny, —He hands her the dough an she's offski.

He lights up another fag.

—We bevvied an gabbed all night. We never noticed Polecat snuck off early. Milky Bar says he declared hisself skint an sloped. When did Polecat ever declare hisself skint

an go hame? Specially when we're all holdin. I mean . . .
no way Polecat would ever leave good company, he knew
we had twenty or thirty each wi at least ten down the sock.
I never thought about it ti the next day.

—Whit d'ye mean . . . never thought about it?
Thought about what? asks Maw.

—Well Crilley goes home an she's dubbed the door
an she's no lettin him in. She's all set to change jockeys
midstream. He climbs up the veranda an the doors open.
He keeks in an there's Polecat lyin bollock on the livin-
room carpet an the telly buzzin away in the corner.

—Polecat's all bruises right down the ribs. He ran out
the house wi his gear under his arm. Crilley battered the
bird a bit an then went to his Maw's for the tablets to top
hisself.

—Fag Maw.

Silence.

Screamin.

Mrs Crilley runs down the lane.

Screamin.

Drinkin from the El Dee.

Runnin.

Screamin.

Drinkin from the El Dee.

I look over an her man's pullin down the blinds.

Cigarette

In the nineteen thirties in Coatbridge, there was a place called the Slap Up. It was all these tenement buildins an narrow cobblestone streets that had been built for Irish immigrants who came to work the Ironworks. A warren of poverty, thirteen people in one room an all that. Crammed in there stinkin; the air was black at night an the daytime sun was always orange.

The Slap Up had a higher population density than New York. The night was lit by the odd gas lamp here an there shinin off the cobbles. The streets were nearly always empty.

At that time all the pubs shut early, say nine o clock. Ma Maw had two aunties, Mary an Lizzie Duffy. They never married. They read books. Maybe they avoided the squalor of motherhood. Most of the men beat their wives an terrified their children as a matter of course. These two used to read the teacups an palms an all that stuff. They never drank . . . uncommon then but they smoked like lums an couldn't go without.

This night they ran out of fags. They were gaspin. It was nine at night, the pubs would be shut an the streets would be dead, dark an quiet.

Jeannie Bogey owned the wee shop down Dundyvan an ye could chap her back door for a midnight loaf or fags or whatever. But this night Mary an Lizzie got there an she never answered. Chap chap chap they're goin an the noise fills the smoky canyons. That was a bit strange because Jeannie Bogey never left the Slap Up unless for a Wake or a Weddin.

So there's Mary an Lizzie pullin their shawls crisscross an pressin through the fog. I can picture them appearin in the light of ghostly gas lamps an then fadin into the mist over an over along Buchanan Street. They never spoke. Makin it through the night without a fag was the only thing in their minds. They would've done anythin for a draw, anythin. They hurried on.

Their shoulders touched automatically when the figure loomed out the fog. They stopped an let it move towards them. The noise of hard feet on the wet cobbles echoed through mist. They couldn't see any buildins, it was so thick. They could've been anywhere . . . for all they knew they could be at the top of some mountain wanderin lost in mist.

The figure materialised. Top hat an tails. They gasped in unison. Immaculately dressed. They were drawn by the intensity of his eyes. Tall. In them days, in the Slap Up, the

79

only place ye would see a suit outside Wakes an Weddins would be in the pawn shop.

—Good . . . evening . . . ladies. He spoke softly without accent or pace.

—G . . . G . . . Good evenin sir, blurts out Lizzie.

—C . . . C . . . Can ye sell us a cigarette please? She curtsied automatic. The man smiled. Mary blushed an looked away peerin into the quiet fog. The only connection with the world was the faint glow of a streetlamp an someone away in the distance singin Whiskey In the Jar. The distant crash of breakin glass.

The man smiled at the sound an so hugely that it began to resemble a grin.

—Certainly ladies, I'll do better than that. I'll *GIVE* you some cigarettes.

Greedy Mary's head swung round to the grin on *GIVE*. The dark hand slid into his inside pocket an produced a solid gold cigarette case. They were mesmerised. It shone an sparked even in the dimness of the foggy night.

CLICK the lid flips open an the insides are padded like a coffin. He pushes it slowly through the darkness between them. Mary's eyes peer over the glitterin edge. It's filled with row after row of cigarettes. He holds it out so they can help themselves. Lizzie curtsies again an delicately slips two from the case. Mary grabs with one hand then the next, stuffin them into the folds of her shawl. It's like the box has no bottom. Her hands are in an out an still there are rows of cigarettes lined up like little bodies. The man laughs an for a moment; his eyes burn with fire.

—Would you ladies care to smoke one with me now, he asks in a voice soft as the priest's. A red star pings in his eye. He cups a gold lighter in his hands an holds it out to

Lizzie first. She puts a fag in her mouth. The three of them are lit up by the blaze of light from the flames. He looks even more impressive an handsome an the skin on his face is a fine surface of fire. Lizzie leans into the flame puffin life into the fag. Mary fiddles with hers in her bony fingers. Lizzie sends a satisfied line of blue smoke burrowin up through the yellow fog into the sky. The lighter clicks them into a further darkness. The man swings around an clicks again. The blaze lights up the grin. Mary notices his breath is stinkin. Fingerin the fag she politely lowers her head into the crucible of light of his cupped hands. Her eyes run down the black silk of his suit. The groin. Pause. The thighs. Pause. The knees. Pause. The razor sharp creases in his trousers take her to his feet.

—JESUS MARY AN JOSEPH

JESUS MARY AN JOSEPH

JESUS MARY AN JOSEPH

JESUS MARY AN JOSEPH JESUS MARY AN JOSEPH JESUS MARY AN JOSEPH

JESUS MARY AN JOSEPH JESUS MARY AN JOSEPH
JESUS MARY AN JOSEPH JESUS MARY AN JOSEPH . . .

She screams into the night; the cigarettes fallin from her shawl trail off into the fog. Lizzie looks at the man an either she's shrinkin rapidly or he's growin. The lighter flickers on his face. Fear breathes in her body. A clip-clop from the cobbles an she looks down an

screams

at the two cloven hoofs stickin out the bottom of his trousers. The man roars in insane laughter. As she starts to run slippin on the cobbles she sees two lumps appearin on his forehead.

They got home an boiled up pots an kettles of water an scrubbed an scrubbed an frantically scrubbed. They washed their mouths out with soap. They sprinkled holy water over each other an round the room. They tied garlic over the door an window. Their clothes stank to high heavens with the stench of his breath. When they burned them, faces of demons an tortured souls writhed in the heat of the flames. Cold sweat. They sat naked holdin each other an shakin. The flames licked off their white skin.

They never told anyone for years an years. They would've been ridiculed an smattered wi guilt. The Catholic community would blame them for drawin the Devil to their doorsteps.

—They were askin for it, they'd say. —What self respectin wummin goes out in the fog after nine askin complete strangers for fags? *EH? TELL ME THAT ? WHAT SELF RESPECTIN WUMMIN . . .?*

Bobby Dunn

Bobby Dunn had got locked up for tamperin wi his sister. The two of them were a bit daft but he got put away. They never let Bobby out. They stuck her away later; kept flashin it out on Bank Street.

Years ago Alice an Pat were walkin up the end of Kirk Street when up comes the bold Bobby. Pat's never met him but Alice knows the whole family. He never looked daft, Bobby, an he only talked a wee bit funny so Pat thought he was just a normal guy.

—Hi yi Alice, goes Bobby. —How's yer Maw?

—Oh she's jist fine Bobby an whit about yer wee sister, is she still in the hospital?

Bobby blushes noddin away like a toy. His sister was

83

in an out the hospital. Mad fits. They never knew that he was touchin her up at the time.

Pat's just started goin out wi Alice an he's tryin to impress – family, friends, usual. He sees Bobby as a candidate an opens this poke of sweets an offers one to him. Here, does Bobby Dunn not go an take the whole packet out Pat's hand an stuffs them into his pocket without even eatin one! Pat's nostrils flare an his muscles tighten. He makes a go for Bobby but Alice's already got hold of him cos she knows what they're both like.

Bobby plods away an Alice tells Pat the score about how Bobby's a mental case an all that. Pat unflares the aul nostrils an congratulates himself on his restraint.

Two months later Pat's at the dancin in St Augustine's chapel hall. In them days the boys asked the girls to dance an if the girl refused ye went an got Big Mick an he chucked her out. So mostly a girl would dance wi any boy. There was the girls lined up at one end of the hall an the boys lined up at the other. Pat looks round an to his left is Bobby Dunn. Alice Riley was the best lookin girl in the hall. She had eyes like winnin the pools. All the boys were terrified of her – she was that beautiful. Long black curly hair, blue eyes an skin white as distemper. Four wide boys were coaxin Bobby to ask Alice up. The music started the slow walk across. People meanderin in an out each other in the darkness, afraid to reach the other end first an afraid to reach it last. No-one went near Alice Riley. Ye needed courage for that. Alice knew. It never bothered her that she was left without a partner the way it bothered Jean Rettie's million freckles an red hair.

But Alice's face near hits the floor when she sees Bobby Dunn makin a bee-line for her. His face is a big grin in the darkness an people are lookin out the side of their eyes to see where Bobby Dunn's goin. Alice's slowly creepin sideways towards the girls' toilet but she's no match for the bold Bobby. He's right there like a homin pigeon.

—Danth, he says.

The whole hall's watchin.

—Pardon, she says leanin over like she can't hear him.

—D'ye want to danth wi me? asks Bobby.

—I . . . I . . . I've got to go to the toilet . . .

—I'll tell big Mick . . . MICK . . . MICK . . .

—I . . . I . . .

Big Mick was already movin out his doorway. He sensed somethin in the air. Jean Rettie was slidin unseen up to Mick's ear an fillin him in on how that bitch Riley refused poor Bobby a dance cos she thought she was too good for him an all this stuff. Out comes Mick's chest an he marches right up to Alice who's tryin to sneak into the girls' toilet but Bobby's got a hold of her dress and she can't get through the door.

Ye can see them arguin across the dance floor. Everyone's dancin but no-one's listenin to the music. Big Mick points to Bobby, who grins, then to the dance-floor an then to the door so everybody knows he's told her to dance wi Bobby Dunn or get out.

The music stops an everyone's eyes are rivets in the dark iron plate of silence. She jerks a nod at Bobby an he scuttles onto the floor. The whole place lets out a sigh an the wide boys are knottin theirselfs. Alice is lookin at the ceiling an Bobby's starin at her lips and breathin on the soft skin of her neck. He's talkin an she's answerin back but she's still lookin at the ceiling. People are sniggerin everywhere. Alice keeps lookin across to Pat but he's ignorin her cos he doesn't want them to think he's jealous of Bobby Dunn.

—*A white spoarts coat ana pink ca arnashun,* Bobby's singin into her neck. Alice is screwin her face up but then she notices he's stopped singin an is actually sayin somethin over an over.

Pat's about to walk away when he sees Bobby wavin somethin in the air in front of Alice's face. It's the bag of sweets.

—D'ye want one of Pat's thweeth? he's askin over an over. Alice is screwin up her face an Bobby Dunn's slabberin down his chin. Big Mick was only half way across the dance-floor when Pat had Bobby Dunn on the floor and was layin the boot in heavy and hard.

Disintegration

I shoulda knew the night she jumped out ma bed an curled into a corner goin

NO NO NO NO NO NO NO NO

NO NO NO NO NO NO NO NO NO NO NO NO

suckin on her thumb. I tried to touch her. I can mind the freckles on her shoulder made her look younger. Like a wean. I tried to communicate but she was wired to the moon.

She sat the best part of an hour. Oblivion. Nothin existed outside the skin of her eyes. Imagine it – right in the middle of a session she goes rigid like a plank an springs me, twice her weight, right off her. She's hung her wee silver rosary beads on the drawer handle. They fell like it was a sign from God or somethin. She claws her way out the bed an folds herself into the corner, knees on her chin. All I could think was the drawer handles must be diggin in her back an the rosary beads diggin into her arse. I already tried to move her but nothin. A lump of wood. Not even the satisfaction of recoil. I cover her wi the blanket to stop her shiverin an shove ma gear on.

Man, I've been down an out – but I never felt lonely like this. I couldn't leave the room. I looked into her eyes. She's starin at somethin soft an comfortin – the hypnotic memory of a toy swingin in a pram, or a white cloud, or her mother's eyes peerin over the edge like two blue moons. She saturated every cell wi one beautiful image from childhood.

I soaked in her beauty. She's silent apart from the odd whimper an suckin her thumb. Any remnants of the old hard-on are long gone an a quiet madness sets in. She's a baby – no more than a year. She's disappeared into the torment an trauma of the fire put there by her brother. A baby surfaced in the flames – the anchor point of innocence – she herself was ice. Fire an ice, the two destroyers fucked into a girl an her fucked into a corner an suckin her thumb an our future fucked by fire or fucked by ice. Every time the fire of her passion rises the ice of repression crushes her. Every time the ice of repression crushes her it crushes me an I die in a fire of desire. But every time she dies twice; she dies of fire an dies of ice. In between these poles is the smallest place in the world where she lives an can never be her; an can never be loved.

Her brother fucked his way into her body, fucked his way into her soul, fucked his way into her heart. Her brother fucked his way into ma life. He fucked his way into ma heart. He fucked his way into ma head. He fucked his way into ma bed an fucked the girl I love into the corner an fucked me onto the window ledge blowin the sad smoke of failure against the flat unseen hardness of the window pane. Birds will die thuddin off glass panes if ye trap them. Their need to soar is greater than their need to live.

A magpie lands an peels the old eye at me but I couldn't give two fucks for any amounts of sorrow now. It could give me all the sorrow in the world – vales of tears an all that shite. This sorrow is bombproof.

Christ almighty, for years an years some cunt was sowin seed after seed of the tentacles that bind the girl I love.

The girl I love was beautiful like a song bird's egg but the egg is cloakin. Inside the smooth blue-sky shell is the blood an guts of a yunk that never formed because some boy on a nest harryin mission punctured the shell wi a rose thorn an put it back in the nest. I came along an held the egg in the palm of ma hand. The blue skies of boyhood shinin down; the shell sprinkled by a lace of stars that fell out the sky every time I looked at her.

She came round an in a cool slow panic, goes, —I'll have to go home. She's gatherin her clothes an mumblin at the same time. It's as if she doesn't know me. I feel like I tried to rape her or somethin. She shuffles into the bog, gets ready, off she pops without even a chirio.

I shoved on some lonely-as-fuck music an cried, first inside then the pressure gave way an the tears rolled out like footballs. I woke up to the dry hiss of speakers an the vastness of four in the mornin. The things we do sometimes. I mind I went out into the garden an lay on the grass. I was cold but this was one broken heart too many. I was at the don't-give-a-fuck-what-happens-to-me stage. I lay there until light. I kept askin the sky what the fuck it's all about. Now an then the silent answers would be punctuated by the tiny delight of a shootin star.

That was the night I learned how to put ma emotions out in space – to put millions of miles between me an pain. I don't know if it's me or ma pain that goes out into the big empty spaces. It's like somethin reaches into ma chest an I feel a liftin. Next thing the pain is gone, suspended for the time. Part of me floats in the realm of gods an part of me squirms on this forsaken surface. A planet where bastards fuck people up an move on plunderin for happiness leavin emotional black holes where the immense gravity of need draws people like me in an disintegrates them.

FUCKIN WHOOSH!!!!!!!!!!!!!!!

Heart broke – nobody gives a fuck. I've had all the gettin left for another man routine an it's sore, don't get me wrong. I've even done the found-ma-wife-in-bed-wi-another-guy bit an that's a big rock in yer heart. When ye get left for someone else there's always hope. But what the fuck do ye do when the girl ye love left ye when she was seven so that ye can never have the full blow-ma-fuckin-mind-moons-an-stars-an-planets-tumblin-out-the-sky love, know? – pavements suddenly rise six inches an ye feel like ye've got clouds on for socks – ye're in LOVE. What do ye do? What do ye do when she's so fucked up she thinks there's nothin wrong cos she can't remember the bad bits then or the bad bits now. What the fuck do ye do in a madness that disintegrates all things in me like an acid ye drink in the mistaken belief it's sweet wine. What the fuck do ye do?

What the fuck do ye do?

What the fuck do ye do?

What the fuck do ye do?

What the fuck do ye do?

What the fuck do ye do?

What the fuck do ye do?

What the fuck do ye do?

What the fuck do ye do?

What the fuck do ye do?

What the fuck do ye do?

What the fuck do ye do?

What the fuck do ye do?

What the fuck do ye do?

What the fuck do ye do?

What the fuck do ye do?

DISINTEGRATE

Granny Harvey

Ma granny used to keep this stuff under the sink.

—Don't yous be goin touchin that, she'd go. —That's the stuff I kill babies wi.

Whenever ye asked if she ever had any boys she said she poisoned them an drowned them cos boys only break a Maw's heart an bring the Polis to the door.

Me an Shamus used to creak open the cupboard door an look at the poison. We never touched it. We stared at it, then at each other, then back at the poison.

—It can go right through yer skin an kill ye, she used to say, —if ye touch it.

It was a big green bottle. All the other bottles under the sink looked dusty an covered in sticky. This one always shone an the label was always bright yella. Away in the back so that ye'd need to reach over the Vim an OMO an Domestos an all that to get it. Sometimes it felt like the bottle was lookin at ye.

Granny Harvey had a face like a pile of jaggy rocks. I mind thinkin all the warts were pencil rubbers. She had millions of warts an her eyes looked from side to side at the top of her sticky out nose. She was terrifyin an her shawl had spiders' webs an leaves an bits of twigs all over it. She slept outside at night an sometimes she had a kip in St Pat's chapel. Her hair was all over the place like grey rain clouds. She wore big man's boots. She was a millionaire everybody says.

Granny Harvey hung about the dark end of the Gas close behind Mutchie's an cadged money off drunk men. That never bothered me an Shamus one bit. We weren't men an we weren't drunk. What bothered me an him was her groggin in yer fish supper. She'd wait till ye were passin an grog right in the chips so ye'd throw it away an then she'd pick it up an eat it. Ye'd be walkin up the Gas close wi yer poke of chips an she'd be pressin into the shadows.

Maybe ye'd see the outline of her face lit up at the edges by the moon.

Ye'd hear this noise like a motorbike startin an then, just as ye reached the end of the close this grogger'd be propelled into the poke. She's stand there wi her walkin stick raised up like she's goin to do damage – crack some skull – we'd be ten or twelve at the time an we'd bolt the course up Kirk Street droppin the chips on the cobbles an chargin through her witchy wailin an laughin.

This night we've got fish suppers each cos Shamus's Maw's won the Snowball. We're comin through the close laughin an shovin white bits of flaky fish in our gubs. The last thing on our mind's Granny Harvey. We gets to the pishy end of the close an,

TULLLLLOCHCHCH

SPLAT!

A big grenner lands on Shamus's half eat special fish supper. Shamus looks like he's goin to go apeshit an attack her. His bottom lip's tremblin. But his anger disappears the minute she whacks him on the head wi the stick. We're off like a bunch of squirrels out a box – crushin the fish suppers wi fear as we get off our marks. Shamus's holdin his head as he skelps Granny Harvey in the face wi his special fish supper. All ye could hear was her laughin an our new shoes slappin an slidin on the cobbles. We looks back an there's the aul hag cricked over holdin her shawl to her belly wi one hand an pickin up the brown chip poke wi the other an her face turned towards us. The steam's hissin off it an more steam's comin out her lips as she starts stuffin the fish an chips in her teethy mouth . . .
shrieking
stuffin fish
shrieking
stuffin fish
shrieking
stuffin fish
shrieking
stuffin fish.
It must've been all over her woolly gloves. We're at the pen close, the other end of the street an she's eatin the fish an pointin the stick at us an laughin. At the same time she's

spittin out bits of the woolly gloves. That's when we decided
to get the aul bastard back.

•

This night me an Shamus's sent to Frank Lungo's for the
chips. At the end of Kirk Street we sees Granny Harvey
loomin about the dark end of the Gas close. Ye've got to go
through the Gas close to get to the chippy. Shamus comes
up wi this plan.

We goes back to ma granny's an gets the big green
bottle out from under the sink. Shamus tims some into a
ready salted Golden Wonder crisp poke.

—Is Frank's shut? goes ma granny from the room.

—No we forgot what we'd to get.

—If ye'd a brain ye'd be dangerous – it's only youse
that's to get out the chippy . . . sent them for cheese an
they fell an skint their knees . . .

She's goin on an on. By this time she's out the room
an meetin us in the lobby an we're tryin to squeeze by her
so's she can't see what we've got. She looks right suspicious
but off we pop into the darkness.

On the telly it says it's the coldest night for thirty years.
It's minus. I sticks ma hands up ma sleeves an pull the sleeves
up theirselfs.

Granny Harvey's still there at the Gas close. She's
swiggin out a bottle an givin it mad starin about everywhere.
We'd usually bolt past but this time we donners right slow,
goin on all the time about how we're gettin pie suppers an
fish suppers an chips an puddins an more chips an right
back through the Gas close to watch the football. She was
listenin cos she moved into the corner like she was invisible

an her eyes stopped movin about.

On the way back up the close ye could hear her startin the motorbike. Shamus slabbered more poison on the suppers. We opened them like flowers fannin the brown paper out. We asked Frank Lungo for hunners of salt an vinegar an brown sauce. Ye could hear Granny Harvey suckin it all up that big beak of hers.

She must've been sloshin that grogger about for ages cos it was the size of a tennis ball as it come through the dark an splattered all over ma very special fish supper.

—Oh look she's spat on ma dinner, I says. She's spat on ma fish supper. Ma SPECIAL fish supper – what can I do? I know! I'll throw it away.

. . . an I drops it neatly on the ground. Shamus leans over an places his on the cobbles. We run wi our heads twisted back an she's stuffin them both in her mouth. Me an Shamus walk home quiet. We don't mention it. It's not every day ye poison somebody.

The next day Shamus an me were chalk white. Aul Granny Harvey was found stiff as a board outside St Pat's.

•

Nearly a year after all that me an Shamus get sent home early from school. We're just in the scullery an he slides across the linoleum an grabs the bottle off ma Granny – who's sluggin it down goodstyle.

—Granny Granny – ye'll kill yerself,

. . . an he slides across the floor an gives the bottle a swipe an it falls smashin on the lino.

—Jesus Mary an Joseph have ye left yer head in the bed this mornin! An how are yous two not at the school?

—Ye'll die if ye drink that . . . Granny Harvey . . . it's . . . it's POISON.

I'm ready to run cos he's about to blurt out all about how me an him kilt Granny Harvey when ma Granny bursts out laughin.

—Poison? Poison, she goes an then she remembers what she used to tell us about it an laughs some more. She thinks an then gets the mop.

—Ay, to some it's poison right enough – but to me it's jist a wee tonic – that's all – a wee tonic.

An she opens the immerser cupboard an in there there's three bottles an she cracks one open an takes a swig.

—Buckfast, she says, best wee pick-me-up in the land.

Me an Shamus stare at each other open mouths an wide eyes wonderin how Granny Harvey died.

Hey for Company

McKraken was this aul man in Old Monkland who used to go down the graveyard every night wi one flower; whatever one was in season.

He had one hand shakin behind his back all the time. Nobody knew what he done down there but rain hail or mist he'd be walkin into the dark. He'd disappear round black edges of tombs an all ye'd hear is footsteps echoed an fragmented by the teethy gravestones.

Jerry Broody showed me him. I was nine. We followed him to the gates an watched him disappear round the tombs. I asked ma Maw about the man wi one hand shakin behind his back an the flower in the other. She says he had an electric shock after his wife died an he never speaks cos he was struck dumb the night he found her wi her wrists slashed on the scullery floor. The blood was spattered on the salad.

When they found him he was sittin on the grass verge in the middle of the M8. He had this cornflakes box turned inside out an he was writin over an over wi a felt tip pen:

Poppies in a green field; flowers on the hillside.
Poppies in a green field; flowers on the hillside.
Poppies in a green field; flowers on the hillside.
Poppies in a green field; flowers on the hillside.
Poppies in a green field; flowers on the hillside.
Poppies in a green field; flowers on the hillside.

He got put in Hartwood for a couple of years.

Ma Maw was right about him bein dumb. The next seven years, me an Jerry Broody must've seen him goin in the graveyard a million times. We called him all the names an threw stones but he never turned round, never spoke, never shouted.

But this night the whole sky's reflectin in ma mad eyes. I've been at his gate all night. I'm steamin. I don't give two fucks what's what. This time I'm goin in the graveyard behind the aul cunt.

His door lets loose a barrage of clicks an fallin chains – Fort fuckin Knox – I flicks the fag in a puddle, a long thin snake of red light hisses as it punctures the surface. I lurks back in the hedges. Trapped water on the leaves comes cascadin down ma chest. It's cold as hell. His bunch of keys thump off the door. I holds ma breath in case he sees steam blowin out the hedge.

He passes. His feet scliff on the pavement. His hand's vibratin behind his back – usual – he's got a rose in his other hand. His coat's wrapped tight an his bunnit's low over his eyes.

He walks at the same pace he always walks. I slides into the orange glow of streetlamps an push through webs of drizzle. I've got the invisible head on cos of the Buckfast an I'm followin private eye style.

—Eh Colombo here, just one more question before I go Mr McKraken. I'm doin ma own jokes now. Mental.

These surges rush through ma body. It's a short walk down Woodside Street to the gates. Before I know it he's in there without even a look round. I skips down an looks round the wall like a cartoon character. I can't help smilin but the smile feels like an insane grin an it frightens me a bit. I whip out Buckie an take a good charge.

—No fuckin problem. Right in there OK, ghosts an fuckin goulies. Here I come ready or not, in yer graves, by one, by two, by three.

In I goes homin in on the scrape of footsteps headin through the tombs.

The orange lights shot over the graveyard wall in sheets but none of the light fell on the stones. It was truly black. I shivered. I tip-toed on the grass avoidin graves. Fuck . . . I nearly caught up wi McKracken.

I'm fifteen feet from the aul bastard an he can't see me. I feel like laughin but ma heart's goin like fuck an ma mouth's like a badger's arse.

He stops at this white stone wi a big angel stickin out the top. This time he's facin me but I've crouched down. It looks like he can see me but he can't. A moon rolls over the wall behind him an the whites of his eyes shine in the reflection from the big angel. It's just him an this stone glowin in the graveyard. Everythin else is black as a pit.

Spooky as fuck.

He bends down an plants the rose somewhere an straightens up. There's a wind gettin up an the twigs are clickin like crabs' legs. I'm thinkin is that it? After all these years is that all there fuckin is? Him bendin down an stickin a flower on his dead wife's grave?

Then,

fuck me!!

. . . does he not start this Indian dance. Round an round he's goin on the grave an murmurin low. It gets louder an louder – he's sayin over an over.

Hey for company, ho for company, happy would I be if a body brought a body spinnin back to me.

Poppies in a green field; flowers on the hillside.

Hey for company, ho for company, happy would I be if a body brought a body spinnin back to me.

Poppies in a green field; flowers on the hillside.

Hey for company, ho for company, happy would I be if a body brought a body spinnin back to me.

Poppies in a green field; flowers on the hillside.

Hey for company, ho for company, happy would I be if a body brought a body spinnin back to me.

Poppies in a green field; flowers on the hillside.

Every time he done a revolution ye could see his fingers shakin in moonlight. He's half bent over. I'm sixteen. I'm out ma face. This is beginnin to scare me. This white frost's formin over the whole place an he's gettin louder an louder. Some cunt out on the main road must be able to hear him. Two wood pigeons flap out the trees breakin branches. He hears nor sees nothin. He keeps right on goin round an round crunchin his feet on the frostin ground an singin out:

Hey for company, ho for company, happy would I be if a body brought a body spinnin back to me.
Poppies in a green field; flowers on the hillside.
Hey for company, ho for company, happy would I be if a body brought a body spinnin back to me.
Poppies in a green field; flowers on the hillside.
Hey for company, ho for company, happy would I be if a body brought a body spinnin back to me.
Poppies in a green field; flowers on the hillside.
Hey for company, ho for company, happy would I be if a body brought a body spinnin back to me.
Poppies in a green field; flowers on the hillside.

Then fuckin

WOOSH!!

This THING pulses up out the ground.
—My God My God I'm goin an can't move.

He's ravin fuckin barkin mad now an he's dancin faster. The thing's all white like the frost an floatin towards him. He looks up an smiles like a half moon's fell out the sky. I'm gravestone still wi terror an they cuddle. Can ye believe it? They fuckin cuddle. His hand's alright now! It's workin it's way up an down this thing's back an all over its arse.

Next thing they move away. He's walkin – she's floatin. They walk down the path like it's a chapel an they're gettin married. They disappear in the fog.

WELL!

I gets up an runs like fuck – slippin every couple of steps. I'm bumpin off gravestones an whimperin like a wee laddie an slippin an crawlin an diggin ma fingers in the grass an pullin masel forward.

The next mornin I'm bruised all over ma arms an legs. I sits on the edge of the bed an lights a fag. I tries to put it down to some crazy dream but I couldn't.

He's still down there every night an the weans are still throwin stones an he's still ignorin them. He's still got one flower an the electric hand. Lookin back it's all crazy. I don't believe it masel. One of these nights I'm goin back down there an then I'll see if I'm really crazy.

Rumplefuckinstiltskin

I was really skint in Sikeside. Some place – plywood windows, dogs an weans everywhere.

This time the Giro's done in.

Drink.

She's fucked off down her Maw's.

The house was warm enough seein as how I'd wired the meter an had electric radiators everywhere. Three in every room – four in the bog. I got them out the Steelwork when it shut down. I was heatin the close for three years an ma bills were only twenty quid.

This time, I might be warm but I'm starvin. I'd the last onion wi an aul bottle of salad cream the night before. I'm smokin ashtray douts an drinkin tea made from a five-day tea-bag.

—Fuck this! I says an pops off to find grub.

I chaps Bonzo's window. He jumps up an gives me the two minutes look. She's goin radio cos he's promised to take her to B an Q. Ye can hear bangin pots an swearin echoin out the close when Bonzo opens the door.

—An I'll not be here when ye get back – CUNT, she shouts, an SLAM.

Here comes Bonzo swaggerin down Sikeside Street.

—Fancy a doss up the canal for spuds?

—Spuds? he goes givin it the question mark look.

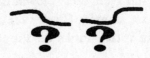

—Ay. I'm cleaned out, not a sausage – Lee Marvin.

He shrugs the shoulders. —I'm gemme.

He rubs his hands an we march off. I feel Liz's eyes drillin in our backs but we don't turn round. I hands him a scrunched up Asda bag an he stuffs it up his jook. The crackling carrier bags sound like poverty.

•

Later on we're comin back along the aul tarmac road. I'm thinkin roast tatties an five day tea. We've got a bag each an he's skinned up. He found a bit in his wee jeans pocket. Survivor of a Persil number one soap sud boil wash. When ye've nothin, next to nothin's a feast. We lights up. I closes the eyes an blows the smoke out over the field like a crop duster, well that's what I'm thinkin . . . when . . .

dust dust dust dust dust dust dust dust dust dust dust dust dust dust dust

whooooooooooooooooooooooooooosh

dust dust dust dust dust dust dust dust dust dust dust dust dust dust dust

. . . up comes this pick-up wi a big red face pressin at the glass. Ye didn't have to ask. Farmer. Spins it round like the films. Ma mouth's still open blowin the last of the smoke out. Ma eyes are amazed. He gets the dust cloud right but the noises are rock chunks an slippin tyres instead of screechin rubber.

The door flies open before the thing's stopped right an he heaves hisself upright.

Up he comes – elbows out – arms swingin – steam comin out his ears – right out the fuckin Beano.

—Get the tatties ower ya perr a ignirnt pigs yees. I sat there an watched yees – the height a cheek howkin ma produce out thon park.

Rantin. Barkin mad. Can't get a word in edgeways. Bonzo's flabbergasted. He's puffin away at the joint – half laughin, half not laughin.

—Ah ken yer faces so a dae. Ah ken yer faces an I'll find out yer names so a will – I'll find out yer names an it's the polis for ye – oh ay – the polis – I've seen yees round here a hunner times an I kent yees were a perr of good for nothin shysters.

He snatches Bonzo's bag out his hand.

A split second stillness that's what I noticed.

It was that freaky quiet when Bonzo does one of two things:

1. Kicks their cunts in.

2. Starts laughin.

He bursts out laughin an Ken Yer Faces goes fuckin ballistic.

—Ya cheeky ignirnt pig, yee steals ma produce an ye've got the lip tae laugh right in ma face. Right in ma bloody face . . . whit kinda world we livin in fur Goad's sake? But I ken yer faces an mark ma words I'll find out yer names – oh ay – don't think ah won't. Right in ma face he's laughin . . . wid ye credit it?

He's stampin in circles. Rumplefuckinstiltskin. I've snuck sideways. Bonzo's creased. Doubled. He's got a hand on the ground stoppin him fallin on his face. Ken Yer Faces comes marchin at me but this is ma dinner. This is roast tatties an five day tea. No fuckin way. He crunches by me on the path an goes to snatch the bag like one of them mail trains that catches the bag whizzin through the station only he's no Flyin Scot an I'm no wooden post. I snatch the bag back violent an give him the snarl. It's a real snarl. I'm not just kiddin to frighten the bastard. Ye can see he's scared. I look crazy as fuck sometimes. Bonzo's dragged hisself off the ground an he's comin over. Ken Yer Faces is runnin round in circles lookin desperate for help.

—*Ya pig, ya big ignirnt pig, them's ma produce mine!!! ma produce . . . mine ya big ignirnt pig ye . . . ignirnt pig, them's ma produce mine!!!!*

On an on he's goin an me an Bonzo's passin the joint rapid an fallin all over the place. We're at the holdin each other an laughin through the nose stage.

107

We'd have laughed all day if Ken Yer Faces never whipped out the knife. A big fold over job – eight inches anyway – like a pocket scythe. *GULP!* I goes.

Bonzo pulls a straight face but I'm in fits still an pointin at the knife wi this crooked finger. Bonzo pulls out his blade. I pulls out mine. Compared to Ken Yer Faces' foldin Claymore they were toothpicks. But Ken Yer Faces doesn't even see them. He's runnin down the hill screamin like he's leadin off an Indian attack. So we hop the hedge an follow, bent over. We're almost parallel an all the time he's screamin back up to where he thinks we are;

—Ye'll no be gettin away ya pair a thievin louts. Ye might hae the produce but ye'll get caught – ye'll hae tae come back for yer caur.

I looks at Bonzo. He looks at me. **What fuckin car?** we thinks at each other. There's this sky blue Escort parked squinty halfway down the hill. Ken Yer Faces is right on it tryin to force the pocket sword in through the walls.

PSHHHHHHHHHHHHHTTTT

—That'll sort yees out, he shouts up an moves to the next tyre.

PSHHHHHHHHHHHHHTTTT

We crouch down vibratin as aul Ken Yer Faces sets about the other two tyres.

PSHHHHHHHHHHHHHTTTT

—Ae . . . the polis'll be here when yees come to get yer motir caur. Hee Hee Hee . . .

PSHHHHHHHHHHHHHTTTT

He's laughin like a Beano character.

When he's sure the exhaust's kissin the tarmac he storms back up the hill shoutin about how that'll teach us an how the polis'll be there when we come to get the car back an if he ever sees us again on his land he'll be well within his rights to blow our arses off wi his shotgun that he just wishes he'd brung that day an in fact he thinks he's got it in the pick up an off he goes runnin.

So do we just in case.

The spuds were great an Bonzo gave me six tea bags some sugar an some tobacco.

When ye've nothin, next to nothin's a feast.

Shootin Star

Ever been in love?

I switches on the wireless this mornin.

— the Cockbridge to Tomintoul road is closed due to heavy snow drifts.

Ever been in love – stone in love – like it's floodin yer body?

Starin out the window. Smokin. Her birlin in ma head. A wooden dancefloor in some castle mibbi. Greensleeves playin an us lockin arms an spinnin.

I'm in this room where ye go for some peace or to impress the priest an nun. The pastoral centre at the college. Full of new birds. First year students. It smelt of girl all shinin in new clothes an make up. An army of Virgins.

They're that shape they'll never be again half between girl an woman – perfect arse an legs but not at the flauntin it games.

Yet.

It wasn't eyes across a crowded room nor nothin. This red hair flitted through the room like a mad paintbrush.

Ten girls for every guy. Ye only needed the right amounts of bits on yer face to be good-lookin. If all the bits were in the right place . . . Man . . . ye were fightin them off – it was a woman swatter ye needed. Away from their mammies the first time an the hormones tricklin through their veins buildin up to a waterfall. Sex penetratin their lectures. Burstin through their ordinary clothes. Nipples poppin at unexpected moments. Naked men surfacin in the middle of their bedside prayers – oiled an gyratin.

Guess how many I had?

Zero. None. Fuck all.

I could kick masel. The right amounts of bits on ma face in the right order. Could've shagged mornin noon an night.

I never.

Why?

I fell in fuckin love . . . that's why.

I'm in the God room pressed up against a million birds. I run ma hand along the piano. Saved me kickin over a chair.

The noise level had went up an the heads returned to normal positions but the eyes were still swivellin in ma favour. I'm checkin out bums an thighs without the Nun seein me.

So I'm sittin there goin plink plonk on this piano – playin the beginin of a hundred tunes like I know them.

This voice snuck up beside me.

—Do you play? she goes . . .

. . . an her breath falls on ma neck. I turns. I don't know what perfume but it pushes its way up ma nostrils like a magic spell.

Red hair. Green woollen jumper. Flowin skirt. Celtic brooch.

—Do I play? I says. Tryin to look modest. Modest? – I had nothin to be modest about. I could play fuck all.

She bats eyes an goes, —Yes, do you play the piano?

—Do you play it?

She lowers her head. —Yes . . . a bit.

Chance to impress, I thinks, sittin down.

She's waitin on me blowin her away. Her head's tilted shy. Hair rushin down her front. Her eyes flit about ma cheekbones an now an then meet mine.

—Here's somethin I wrote masel.

—You write music? She claps her hands an bounces up an down like a primary five wean. I mind smilin an takin a closer look at her face.

—No . . . not really I make wee tunes up . . . sometimes . . .

How the fuck was I to know her Maw was a music teacher? I bangs out a C wi each hand an changes to a G wi a couple of variations.

—Did you write that yourself? She tries to smile but looks like her horse just died. —Can I have a go?

Fuck me. The place went silent. Dead. Fields of Athenrye. She's got this voice. Jee . . . sus I'm watchin her mouth openin an shuttin. Mesmerised.

I falls in love. Suddenly I'm beamed up like Star Trek an the universe is massive. There was this College trip to

Tomintoul an fuck me if we're not stone in love by the time we get there. We never slept all weekend. All night long we weaved under the stars – bright as fuck up there.

That's how every time the radio's electric breath spits out about how the Cockbridge Tomintoul road's shut it rips through me like fire.

Tomintoul.

I thought I was in love before we got there but fuck me.

I mean.

It was Easter snow. We're up this hill away from every cunt. We made a snowman an stuck a smile on his face wi stones; wrapped her red an yellow scarf round his neck an sticks ma bunnit on his head. I can see us now, laughin, holdin each other up.

The Easter snow's faded to fuck all now an I feel like ma heart's been shredded on rocks an ma blood sucked into the clay.

We're kissin this time an the mornin sun's shinin on our shoulders. Or the evenin wind's breathin out spring flowers an fuckin pine trees. At night the sky's a million starry eyes winkin. The whole Universe knows our secret.

Even when other cunts were there it was weird. I watched her pickin the guitar an singin – it's like the last ever song. Adam an Eve.

Her fingers are stick insects on tightrope strings strummin the wires holdin ma heart back from explodin. Fuckin BOOM blood everywhere but still smilin.

That night we left the buildin. There's her face formin in the glistenin light of stars. Walt Disney film. Bambi could've jumped out the trees or Snow White or the Dwarfs an we wouldn't have batted an eyelid. We're gazin up.

Ma head's doin overtime. I'm lookin at the stars thinkin the maddest stuff. If we put all the poets that ever lived onto the job of namin all the stars wi perfectly precise names we'd still not know what they were all about. Right at that fuckin moment I realises ma love is more than that – fuckin gigantic. Frightenin. We sighed into the big empty spaces between them.

See if all they stars crash down an two moons glowed in the sky it'll make fuck all difference now. I'm mad wi it. I keep seein her walkin in misty mornins an all that shite. I know it's poofy but that's what happens an usually Greensleeves is playin – an orchestra behind trees? I hate musicals too.

Daaaa daa da da daa daa daa da da daa daa daa da daa daa da . . .

She's smilin. Her hair's blowin over these stupid lookin green hills. But Tomintoul was real. It really happened even if it's not true.

We're one shadow this night, isolated on a wee bridge. Suspended in between water an star-music. Closest to heaven we'll ever be. But all the time ma minds sayin,

—Get to fuck out of this, get to fuck out of this.

I knew it. Heart breaker. Too fuckin late. Devil an the deep blue sea. We're a planet orbitin other planets. Like God let us out where no cunt's been before.

An the stars' distance brings it home. BANG. Star after star after star. Paradise separated from paradise separated from paradise. No cunt can change the stars. If we were stars . . . but we're not.

Dawn. Were beside this pool. It's calm as fuck. An so

are we. Tree tops reflect on it like roots grabbin at the water, sky, water, sky. We lean into its topsy turvy world an one thing seems to be another. An our love's the same – one thing to us an somethin else to every other cunt.

We let that pain in. Fuckin eejits. I wanted to take their love away. Oh ay! Think twice about drivin between us then. We end up wi big empty gaps for hearts. An nothin can fill them an I'm standin wi all this fuckin love an nowhere to put it. I knew it'd destroy me.

She's squeezin ma hand an I'm thinkin in one pool or another our love'll drown, unnoticed as funeral tears. The wind skates the surface, condemns the pool to be ice, to be frozen, to be smashed an splintered.

Ma life was wiped out before – winds frostin through me like glaciers. Empty fuckin canyons. Lost – almost dust. I makes this comeback. No drink. No drugs. Does it all right. An what? I'm almost dust again.

Fuckin yahoo!

The ripples on the pool. No rehearsal in this life. Straight on – straight off. An we're givin this chance up to fear. Ma thoughts are black as fuck now.

Loss.

The universe moves a million waves across a million puddle surfaces an a million hearts are ripped out every day. I toss this stick tryin to make some difference an ma waves are gone in a second.

But she kisses me. Sticky mouths, fingers in red hair and minglin breaths. Now the universe is spinnin wild an fuckin weird. Mental. She laughs.

—This is brilliant, she goes.

Green eyes. Blue eyes. Land an sea. Welded thegether. Wild fuckin horses couldn't part us – but they did. Fuck

115

sake – the wee world outside the Universe inside us dragged us apart.

I can still taste her. Virgin's lips. The dew on her hair an in the creases of ma skin.

Rain.

Pock pock pock   Pock pock

pock   Pock   pock pock

Pock   pock   pock

Pock   pock pock   Pock pock

pock   Pock   pock pock Pock

pock   pock

Pock   pock

                    pock

On the pool movin out in circles. We have to go home. I feel the stones are goin to cry in pain if I don't. Millions of years old. I thinks – a billion years blacker than us – an sometimes I felt a billion years darker than her.

There's this stream, clear as an angel's soul. Last year's on the bottom. Leaves, dead insects an stuff. Forgotten. I tell her she'll never be forgotten in me an she squeezes ma hand. An this year'll fall an float helpless an sink. I looks in the stream at her lookin back. Fuck me, she's ma reflection so that I can't see me without her. If I do I feel like a leaf or a stone on the bottom of a pool. She's singin.

116

—My young love said to me
my mother won't mind
and my father won't slight you
for your lack of kind.
She stepped away from me
and this she did say,
it will not be long love
'till our wedding day.

It floats downhill. An there's me wishin it was like that for us. No chance!

Way below on a wet shinin road the others are windin away. They're wonderin where we are. Where've we been all night? The Nun's been keepin an eye on us. Some eye. Looks the other way an

whoosh . . .

. . .we're off in the dark. I don't think of God much but love does yer head in. On this hill He's writin this song for me an her. The mouths of turnin birds twistin a tune over the mountain.

—Brilliant, she goes, clappin. The rush of river far below an the wind fracturin on trees an the clouds goin dark light dark light dark light in time is our emotions. I turns an kisses her light on the cheek. Fuck me – ye can say that much not sayin nothin. Then ma head's brung all the animals into the orchestra. Rabbits are thuddin out the rhythm. The whole song's composin itself. We kissed an closed our eyes on the world – the song played. Weird an wild. Ma head's sayin it's goin to be played someday usin the fuckin trees as aerials to God. By that time me an her an every other cunt'll be dust blowin about on one wind.

117

WHAM!!!

The sky's black as fuck. Were kissin. I sees this shootin star through ma eyelids. I opens ma eyes,
whizzzzzzzzzzzzzzzzzzzzzzzzzzzzzzzzzzzzzzzzzzzzzzzzzzzz
. . . it goes, lightin the tops of the pines. Were pressed against this wire fence an she's facin the wrong way. What happened next shocked me an I still can't believe it to this day but it really happened.

—Did ye see that? I goes.

She spins round lookin about into the different darkness.

—Christ! a shootin star right across the sky – whizzz – ye shoulda seen it, ye coulda made a wish, so ye could.

She looks kinda sad an we both knew the wish. I don't know why I done this but this feelin of power came over me. Half jokin, half serious. I says,

—Do ye believe in God?

She nods her head so I turns her by the shoulders an this is exactly what I says.

—God, we never seen that shootin star ye sent us there could ye send us an . . .

Fuck me!!!!

Whooshhhhhhhhhhhhhhhhhhhhhhhh

Right across the sky. Darkness lights up like daylight. This gigantic shootin star right to left across the Grampians.

—*Oh my God. Oh my God. Oh my God. Oh my God. Oh my God. Oh my God. Oh my God. Oh my God. Oh my God. Oh my God. Oh my God. Oh my God. Oh my God. Oh my God,* she's goin, an runnin up the path an runnin back down an lookin at me in wonder an lookin at me in fear an thinkin I'm mad an thinkin she's mad an thinkin I'm God. I'm in shock. If ever I believed in God totally it was standin in the bars of light that pushed through the dark tree trunks that night. Ma head's goin,

 —Fuck me! enough faith to move stars but not to be thegether.

 An this surge of words comes into ma head.

 —In space an time, I'm a shootin star that missed her by inches an crash landed in a vale of fuckin tears.

•

We held hands all the way home in the mini-bus – scared of any distance at all. It was our fingertips said goodbye. Christ. I'd rather die than that again.

 —Ride on.

 That's all I could think of to say to her. It's an Irish song. Fuckin ride on.

The Big Empty

I mind the night I flung Carmen in the canal. We were at Stars an I'd been talkin to this bird that she went to school wi. I never thought nothin of it.

Outside I'm breathin in November air deep an cool in that way ye can only do when ye're pished. I smell her comin up to me an I levels the head but she's starin up the sky an blowin up her fringe.

—Oh oh trouble I says – trouble – so I tries to throw the arm round her. She spins out of the hold before I can smack the lips on her an clip clop clip clop she goes wi folded arms an smoke smoke smokin away at a Club king size. She swayed from side to side wi the smoke comin out at regular intervals. Steam train. Sex.

—Whit the fuck's up now, I goes but ma words zoom
by into the West End Park an bounce off the flats shatterin
like Buckfast bottles an showerin down through the clip
clop smoke smoke puff puff folded arms an wigglin arse.
She's faded into the darkness so I makes after her.

—For fucksakes wait, I'm shoutin an followin her
movin shadow.

BUMP

I'm that drunk I bumps right into her. I sees the red light of
her fag comin at me. I jerks the head down quick.
Hissssssssssssssssssssssssssssssssssssssssssssssssssssssssssss.

The smell of singed flesh. I slaps the hand on ma
forehead.

—Aaaaaaaaaaaaaaaaaaaaaaaaaaww what the fuck did ye
do that for?

—Go an get the wee tart Puff if ye want her. Puff
puff.

—What? I'm rubbin spit into ma forehead.

—That wee fuckin tart. Go'n shag her, she's a fuckin
slut anyhow.

—Who the fuck are you on about?

—You fuckin know fine well. That Harriet the chariot
that's who. Pressin her tits up yer arm an slidin her thigh up
yours. Thought I wasn't lookin. Thought I couldn't see.
Oh but I was lookin so I was.

Fuck me. Caught rotten.

—Was she fuck, I goes. You are fuckin crazy, so ye
are – you need help – know that? It's the fuckin loony bin
you should be in, so it is.

She starts pullin at her hair wi two hands an grittin
her teeth. He voice is squeezin out the gaps. Hartwood.

—Don't call me mad. Don't call me mad. Don't point call point me mad point.

Then she starts sayin it over an over an all the time diggin her finger in her own chest. Ye can hear it thumpin in the dark.

Don't thump call thump me thump mad thump. Don't thump call thump me thump mad thump. Don't thump call thump me thump mad thump. Don't thump call thump me thump mad thump.

—She wasn't anywhere near me.

—Don't thump call thump me thump mad thump.

—She was at one end of the table for Christsakes – an I was at the other end.

—Don't thump call thump me thump fuckin thump mad thump.

She's clenchin her fingers into ma shoulders now.

—We were only talkin.

—Don't call me mad Don't call me mad Don't call me mad Don't call me mad Don't call me mad Don't call me mad Don't call me mad.

I decides to go for the calm-her-down approach.

—Look, I love you. What the fuck would I want wi a wee slut like that?

—What the fuck would ye want. Huh. Shag her, that's what.

I wouldn't go near **her** wi a barge . . . I thought I had her but she's right in there sharp as a tack.

—So ye'd go near other birds then?

—No . . . I . . .

—If ye wouldn't go near **her** wi a barge pole well there must be birds ye would go near wi a barge pole. Who is it?

Eh? Who the fuck is it?

She's shakin me back an forward an the nails are diggin in so I rips maself away an starts walkin.

—See, can't take the truth. Hoor maister.

HOOOOOOOORMAAAAAAAISTER!!!!!!!

She's shoutin loud as fuck an ye can see the shapes of punters comin out the dancin strainin through the web of streetlight to see where the commotion is but all they can see is the blackness of the middle of the park where we're standin an the disembodied voices like ghosts that never quite found heaven doin battle in eternal jealousy.

—I never even noticed she was into me. If I did I'd've got to fuck out her road.

—Ya bastard . . . ye wanted to fuckin shag her . . . didn't ye? Didn't ye? Ye wanted to fuckin shag her!!!

—See you – you are fuckin crazy.

ZIIIIIIIIIIIIIIIIIIING!!!!!!!!!!!!!

Aw fuck me, she bangs the head right on me. I can see fuck all. Cunts are shoutin abuse from the edge of the park an I hear her feet crunchin into the grass as she runs. All the time she's shoutin

HOOOOORMAAAAISTER!!!!

over an over an it's gettin smaller an smaller in the direction of the canal.

HOOOOOOOORMAAAAAAAISTER!!!!!!!

HOOOOOOOORMAAAAAAAISTER!!!!!!!

HOOOOOOOORMAAAAAAAISTER!!!!!!!

HOOOOOOOORMAAAAAAAISTER!!!!!!!

HOOOOOOOORMAAAAAAAISTER!!!!!!!

I get ma eyes open an sees the yellow streetlights. It's

all like it's underwater cos ma eyes are spinnin an ma nose is throbbin an nippin like fuck at the same time. Ever been fucked right on the beak? It's no fun. I starts runnin towards her.

—Right that's it ya fuckin bastard, I'm shoutin.

But she's cute. She keeps a step out ma reach. I'd've done her in an she knew it. She kept runnin in short bursts to the canal an callin me all the wankers an hoormaisters an dicks under the sun.

I wanted to choke the life out her – slow.

Then I had an idea.

All the life I'd had flashed before ma eyes an I never liked none of it. All the life I'd had wi her flashed in front of ma eyes an I never liked none of that. This blackness flooded into me. A darkness was radiatin out ma spine an ma insides were feelin like a fridge. I was clear what I had to do. I decided to do maself in. I decided to jump in the canal.

—That's it – I'm in the canal. I've had enough of this shite. Just you watch this. This is somethin ye're never goin to forget. Ye'll be fuckin sorry so ye will.

I waited for her to run over an slobber me wi kisses but does she fuck. She starts rippin up clods of turf an flingin them.

—Jump Fuckin jump ya waaaanker. Fuckin waaaanker. Waaaaaanker. WAAAAAAAAAAAAANKER.

They must've heard her screamin at The Fountain. They must've heard her screamin in every house in the Brig.

—WAAAAAANKER, she's goin loud as an aeroplane. The lights in the flats are switchin on an off an curtains are twitchin an voices an peerin eyes on the edge of the park are submergin into our black world. I starts to march at the canal. I'm sayin nothin now. She's eggin me on all the time.

Through her teeth she's sayin, —Jump jump ya bastard I can't wait . . .

I can see canal bridge. I looks up. The stars are gettin closer all the time. Ma breath's billowin out an tornadoin up to heaven. Ye can smell the rancid canal banks. I light ma last fag so as she'll know I mean business.

She's stopped shoutin now. She's hissin low an the lights are goin out in the flats an the curtains stop twitchin an the murmurin edges of the park become lines of yellow light onto black an the voices laugh an giggle their way to warm beds an condoms.

I'm surrounded by night. The night's crept inside me too an it's cold inside ma skin. She's off the grass. The click click of her heels begins on the path. I mind steadyin maself comin off the grass. It's easier to walk on grass than concrete when ye're pished.

She thinks I won't do it. She's got folded arms an puffin away darin me. I looks over the bridge an back in her eyes. There's no words now. It's all or nothin. If I don't do it she'll clip away there singin some stupid fuckin song that's got nothin to do wi what's goin on an yet it's got everythin to do wi what's goin on. Roll out the fuckin barrel or somethin. But I've got somethin in ma favour this time. It's been lodged in ma head for months now – the canal. I've seen it before. Ye think of some mental things when ye're drunk. Maybe ye don't do it that night an ye don't do it the next few times ye're out yer face. When ye wake up in the cold light of day ye say, thank fuck I never done that – jump off the flats – drive a car full steam ahead through the Polis station window – run bollock up the Main Street – jump through Asda's plate glass window – run round Asda's wreckin the joint – walk along the main street on a Saturday afternoon smashin all the shop windows – an millions of other stuff that comes into yer head like a good idea when ye're pished. So she knows fuck all about this bein a plan.

She screws up her face when I struggle up onto the wall. I'm tryin to get balanced cos it's one of them walls that's got a pointy bit at the top. Fuck me I nearly fell in tryin to stand up straight. I mean what's the point of doin yerself in if ye're goin to look stupit as fuck in the process. I can see she's scared. She's holdin the fag an exact inch from her lip. Paralysed. I needed somethin good to say, last words an all that but all I could think of was – you ruined ma fuckin life. I was goin to say right after that —tell the world I'm sleepin in the stars – an then recommend a song for ma funeral but I slipped. I glimpsed her face as I sunk into the black November air. She looked like one of them characters out the Beano when they go – GULP.

So did I. On the way down a lot of things happened. Ye'd think nothin much could happen in twenty feet but time went dead slow. Ma coat flung itself back up at the wall like it never wanted to jump, like it was taken by surprise. So was I.

Every time ye talk about suicide some cunt says — what if ye jumped off the flats an on the way down ye changed yer mind? – I mean what do ye do, phone a fuckin taxi? I used to think people like that were pricks but here am I rattlin down at the cold canal warp factor five an I've changed ma mind the minute I slipped off the wall. Yer mind works fast as fuck. I'm thinkin all this an suckin the aul breath in on the way down so as I can stay alive till I resurface. It seemed like an hour before Carmen let out the big scream. An it seemed like another hour before I surged into the water.

First thing was I nearly broke ma fuckin legs. The water's only four feet deep. Crumple I went an I'm under for a millisecond. I shot back up wi all the white water fallin off me like a rocket. All kinds of birds an stuff are flappin like fuck out ma road an I suppose the sleepin fishes exploded, duntin off the canal bank in the process. The cold hits me like a fuckin lightenin bolt made of ice. I'm some weight seein as how bein dressed for the dancin is not the best way to be dressed in a canal in the middle of winter in the middle of the night.

Most of the ice is only a millimetre thick. I'm tryin to make for the edge an takin sharp breaths when I sees her in her disco dancin gear cloppin down the stairs. I don't know where I gets the courage but under I goes for twenty seconds. When I surface she's roarin —I'm sorry I'm sorry I'm sorry . . .

After I clear the water from ma eyes I can see she's roarin. She's runnin up an down the canal-bank searchin the water – tryin to look through its black surface wi her black eyes an shoutin —Please please God I'll do anythin I'll do anythin.

I'm clingin to the rushes at the edge an, even though I'm freezin I'm lovin it. I'm lovin it for two reasons: 1. She loves me; 2. I've got her roarin an cryin.

Sometimes when I'm at a wake I just burst out laughin at the Rosary. So here's me hidin in the canal. More likely to freeze to death than die from the fall an I start laughin. She's sobbin. First it's like a dog sniffin an she stops cos she's scared but then off she goes again.

—Oh God don't let him die don't let him die.

HAHAHA   HAHAHAHAHA

HAHAHA   HAHAHAHAHA
HAHAHAHAHA

I can't stop laughin. I'm nearly drownin cos I'm bendin over wi it. I soon comes to ma senses when the water around me starts goin up like the General Belgrano. Sploosh sploosh it's goin. She's launchin brick after brick at me. I drags masel out the water like a wet Labrador, takin a couple of bricks on the back an starts chasin her down the canal into the distance.

She's back to callin me a wanker an all this stuff an every now an then she's bendin an lobbin a brick over her shoulder as she's runnin. It took me longer than usual to get a hold of her dodgin the bricks. But when I did I was that fuckin mad I launched her in the canal. I never wanted to kill her. I wanted to see her face when she hit the water.

She can't swim.

But she's not slow the bold Carmen. No sir. I'm waitin for the splash an peerin in the dark when I feels this tuggin at ma leg. Next thing I'm howked off ma feet. She's grabbed ma leg on the way down an there's the two of us in the water.

She's out like a shot. I'm under the water an movin about like the SAS. Every time I comes up she's fuckin me wi bricks an shoutin abuse about ma family. Eventually I gets up in the reeds. She knows I'm in there somewhere but she's launchin the bricks at the wrong bit. I waits till I hears cryin. She strikes a match an I think —how the fuck are they still dry?

The light from the match flares a big circle round her an I think how she looks like an angel. I'm breathin onto the canal surface so's it'll mingle wi the slab of mist. She's blowin the smoke up the sky an ye can hear drip drip as the water runs out her clothes. She starts scrunchin along the ash road in the direction of the yellow lights an every now an then I sees the red glow of her fag at her head followed by the arc tracin down to her waist an then back up wi the next draw.

I waited till I heard the distant click click of her feet on the pavement an her disappearin down Blairhill Street. I slithered out the canal like a slimy eel. Ma fags were soaked. I chucked them. It sounds mad but I vaulted the wall an forgot that it was twenty feet at the other end.

Fuck ye! Down I goes tumblin through the trees an landin winded on the hard roots. I tried to get up but I conked out. Must've lay there hours cos when I woke up ma gear creaked when I tried to move. Frost. I looks at maself. I was like the fuckin ice man. If any cunt hada seen me they'd've ran a mile – me creakin out the blackness all white like a spook. An I was gaspin for a fag. Creak creak I'm goin along the path.

Ye can hear how quiet the town is. The odd car buzzes into the silence an fades. The aul teeth are goin chitter chatter ninety to the dozen an I can't stop them.

That was when it happened. Ye'd think I'd remember that night mostly for jumpin in the canal an then throwin her in but that's not it. This feelin went into me. A big fuckin empty feelin. Right through me like a glacier it went an I starts to run to get away from it. How daft can ye get? There's this feelin inside me an I'm runnin to get away from it. Fuckin stupid. Anyway the last thing I believe in is God an all that shite. But I'm runnin through these trees like a maddie an all the twigs are slashin in ma face an I feels the sting but I don't cry out nor nothin.

Then I'm on ma knees. I'm on ma knees an I'm lookin up to the sky like some cunt out a bible-thumpin film.

—*If there is a God,* I'm goin —if there is a God fuckin help me, I shouts all stuff like that loud as fuck up at the stars and then I burst our greetin like a big lassie. Thank fuck no cunt was there. Ye could never live that down in the Brig – the two worst things – believin in God an cryin like a big lassie. There was no flashes of light, no voices, no good feelins. I stopped cryin an walked creak creak to the road. The only miracle was the taxi that drew up soon as I stuck ma hand out.

All the way down the road I'm thinkin of Carmen. How I'm goin to beg ma way into the house an beg ma way into the bed – not to shag her – it's one of them cases when ye just want to hold onto someone. In fact I wanted to be inside her. Ma whole body inside her's away from the world.

—Cold? asks the taxi driver cos he hears ma teeth chatterin. I mumbles somethin that meant I'm-too-drunk-to-talk an he shut up. But I can feel the water runnin off me onto his good seats so I asks him to drop me ten houses away from mine. I hands him two quid. When he gets it he sees it's wet. By this time I'm out the taxi an offski over the gardens.

—Ya fuckin bastard get back here, he's shoutin an — Tango Tango, he's screamin into the radio to get his taxi mates round to kick fuck out me.

But I'm burrowin into the dark an at ma own back door before ye know it. The door's open. That's unusual I thinks cos she usually locks the lot an I've got to sleep outside. I sneaks in an wham the heat hits me like a hammer. I throw all ma gear off. I mind it slappin down on the linoleum floor an I'm warm right away. Ma skin's nippin wi the heat. I sneaks bollock up the stairs an opens the room door. The window's open an a cold wind's blowin in. The bed is untouched an empty. I'm on ma own. Fuck me, there I goes again. I fling maself on the bed goin —God help me God help me, over an over cryin loud like a madman. Outside the commotion of taxis arrivin lights up the night an fills the air wi threats. Fuck them all.

H

(For Jig a Jig who died in 95)

I've got a Magic Charismatic Leopard. He's five feet high. He's lime green like teddy-boy socks wi big black spots all over. He wears a pair of pink sunglasses an he is coooool.

Sat him in the front seat, clunk click. Got some looks; big laughs. Weans waved an jumped up pointin. Maws slapped an dragged them off – faces twistin back to see the car.

Ma wee nephew gave me it. He sat it in the front seat an done a bunk – not a word. Next thing I noticed, this leopard's got powers. I goes out to the car this mornin an he's smilin in a million raindrops on the windscreen. I'm on a downer. I don't want to but this smile spreads across ma face like a Cheshire cat.

I clunks an clicks us in. ZooOOooOOoom – offski.

I'm drivin an talkin to this leopard. Free shrink. Never charged me nothin. I decides he needs a really good name. I mean, what's in a name? A lot – that's what.

This night it's Hartwood. Visitin Big Danny. Weird fuckin place so it is. First thing's the high fence on the railway bridge to stop them jumpin.

The last time Danny's been on the drink. He's not to get out. Me an Davie plumps ourselfs on his bed. Danny's on a right downer so we draw him out slow. He grunts an rolls onto his elbow. His belly flops onto the bed before he comes to rest. He lights up. Inhales. Blows the smoke like a mad cherub slanty up the yella room.

I knew Danny was pished but he's not lettin on.

—How've ye been big fella?

—Aw fuck me man . . . it's slow in here . . . whit a fuckin drag . . . these cunts get me down . . .

His hand sweeps the room like some Mafia boss.

—Fuckin loonie tunes!!!

he shouts an cough-laughs flat onto the bed. His belly's tryin to find a centre of gravity. He looks pregnant wi somethin big. The other loonies are hidin from the big man an a silent sadness paints itself into the walls.

Danny falls asleep.

We leave.

This time's different. Davie sits in the back cos Green Leopard isn't for movin. Davie cracks a smile an our three crazy grins follow the headlight beams into the east.

Fuckin sad – this bleak track above Glasgow is the last scene cunts see before gettin dubbed in Shotts or Hartwood.

Victorians used to fuck ye in the loony bin for pickin

yer nose or scratchin yer arse. Yer family'd be black affronted ye were cookie boo so they made sure nut houses were in nowhereseville. I'll tell ye somethin ye don't get a more out the way joint than this moor. Spoo Key!

This night we're laughin. The rain's beltin on the road like six inch nails nailin the tarmac to the moor an the cats eyes are starin, rows of Hari Kari cat's heads comin at us through the storm.

Shotts jail's drizzly through orange lights like an American Penitentiary. Concrete's a good servant but a bad master, I'm thinkin.

Davie's always thinkin the same as me so I goes, —at least they cunts know when they're gettin out Davie. When the fuck's big Danny gettin out?

He's starin out the window cos he feels one of ma tirades comin on.

—I'll tell ye when – when the doctors an nurses stop playin fuckin God. I mean, they know a lot about somethin the human race knows fuck all about. I mean ye fling a cup off a wall – Bang – five years added on. Not a fuckin judge or court in sight just some specky bastard just out the doctor school. We'd be better off lettin that mad Leopard say who's in an who's out. I'm sure the Leopard nodded.

H

Hartwood Hospital.
Asylum.
Victorian.
Long   dark   empty   windows
f r i g h t e n i n s a n d s t o n e

Green Leopard blinks an smiles. He's goin to like this.

Clunk clunk clunk – we leave the car. The gloom lifts. Ye have to buzz at the door. The attendant lets ye in if ye don't look mental. So he thinks two grown men holdin up what looks like a drunk, lime green, black spotted, pink sunglassed Leopard in the icy Shotts night-time is normal.

Buzzzzzzz – we're in.

The blast of heat hits us wi his broad grin.

—Hi ay, he says, noddin like he had a Leopard the exact same five minutes ago.

There's pish in the air. A long long corridor disappears to Ward One.

Patients creep up an are gone like ghosts into nooks an crannies discovered decades ago. Me an Davie are lookin through a membrane of reality coverin all different perspectives. Silence presses on us from all angles.

Leopard's magic starts workin. Laughin twists an echoes out shadows. Eyebrows lift. Eye whites show. Faces creak to smiles. Plenty missin teeth – way to go here. Tombstone City in every cunt's mouth. Loppin tongues an squeaky gums. We gather this army in the two hundred yard walk. The subtle commotion of slidin slippers permeates the membrane. Heads poke out of all manner of portals. Staff an patients are laughin. It's like the voltage goes up in the lights an the whole buildin smiles. Leopard is a Messiah wi his buzzin disciples shufflin an mutterin in tongues an gums an slabbered lips. Me an Davie are bearers.

This big laugh fires up like a passin jet. A wide eyed pause an the dance continues. Big Danny bellows at us an the Leopard. He's sober an tuned into our madness.

Ward One. We leave our disciples pressin the glass like a mad disassembled totem pole. We meet the usual. Fred Heathcliffe says his polite —Hello Mick hello David how are you this week, an pushes his head politely forward waitin for an answer. He sees Leopard an smiles. —And who might this be then?

—He's our new pal Fred. D'ye like him? We're lookin for a name for him, Fred . . . he needs a good name . . . he's a good guy, so he is.

Fred ambles off promisin to tell Danny soon as he gets the right name.

Fred's Maltese. Don't know much but I'm sure when he was seven an swingin in some park in Malta, by no mad stretch of the imagination could ye predict he'd end up in an asylum in cold North Lanarkshire.

—Davie, I am Heathcliff, he goes this night tryin to explain.

When he talks about Cathy it's real tears. But this night he's smilin. Magic Leopard sees to that.

John – Byzantine expert – says he lives in the New Houses near Davie. They're forty years old. This nut-job Billy almost attacks ye by runnin at full tilt an stoppin short, clenched fist raised. He's been doin that fifteen years. No cunt flinches no more.

Up comes Jig a Jig waddlin.

—*SWEET SWEET*

—We've none.

—*CIGARETTE CIGARETTE.*

—None.

Danny chucks a fag. Jig a Jig pulls the bottom lip out at Leopard an shoots off holdin the fag at the burnin end, mumblin. He's Pakistani, Ethnic Cleansed from Uganda by that mad bastard Amin in the sixties. Scotland's where he came. Lost it before touch down. Been here since. What nightmares hurl behind his two-word language of SWEET

SWEET an CIGARETTE CIGARETTE?

We took Danny out through energy an laughter. They waved. Danny made the lime green, black spotted, pink sunglassed Leopard wave back.

Lucky we had Green Leopard cos Hartwood sticks ye on a downer. It's the buildin an the atmosphere. We fuckin mad or what? Victorian hangovers.

Big Danny's callin the other loonies all these names – he's got a different voice for each word like every word was said by a different person. Spoo Key.

Idiots, eejits, dafties, lunatics, *mentally disordered,* insane, **mad,** lunatic, moonstruck, of unsound mind, not in one's right mind, *non compos mentis,* deprived of one's wits, d e r a n g e d , *demented,* certifiable, mental, abnormal, psychologically abnormal, *sick,* mentally disturbed, mentally ill, of diseased or disordered or distempered mind, unbalanced, brain-damaged, ravin mad, stark ravin mad, *mad as a hatter,* mad as a March hare, off one's rocker, gaga, loony, declared insane, certified, mental . . .

AWAY WI THE FUCKIN BONGOS!!!

We took him to his Maw's. Had a bit of a crack. She said Pink Panther as a name – I mean c'mon – a fuckin lime green Leopard called the Pink Panther? Is she mad or what? All the road back Davie an me fired likely names out. None fitted. The sky cleared an stars were out. The cat's eyes looked more sane. We gets back at Hartwood at eleven. The Leopard's grinnin at the moon.

Danny goes, —night Mick, night Davie.

He leans in the car, lifts up one of its ears an whispers,
—'Night Hartwood, to the Leopard.

Me an Davie turn to each other an laugh the way ye
laugh when ye've discovered the perfect name.

—Night Danny ma man.

Next week.

BZZZZZ. The door opens. Danny waves. Click. The
door shuts. We zoom off past dark windows interrupted
here an there by pale moonlit faces. Some wave at the
Leopard, others stare until our tail lights disappear.

I've got a Magic Charismatic Leopard. He's five feet
high. He's lime green like teddy-boy socks wi big black spots
all over. He wears a pair of pink sunglasses an he is coooool.
His name is Hartwood.

Note not Included

Hard as fuck our Joe. Cunt of a childhood, Children's panel, doins, ran away from home hunners a times, courts, fights, knifes, burglaries, lifted in Scotland, Blackpool, Ayr, Airdrie, London, Utrecht, Hamburg, Inverness, Coatbridge, Wilhemshaven, Hull, more fights, drink, drugs, more fights, two wives, divorce, more divorce, more drink, women problems, fights, drug problems, weans, flittins – couldn't settle.

He's hard . . . not cos he could fight – he was hard cos he got hisself out all that shite . . . he straightened out his life.

I'll never forget the time he burst out greetin cos I said I loved him. Just like that, the tears are runnin down his face an he can't look. He's over at the window still. Quiet. Tryin to get it thegether. Takin breaths an I'm kiddin I don't notice.

When he turns ye can see the tear marks, like varnish an he smiles an goes;

—Time ye got that fuckin grass cut. I can't see aul McGinty gettin her gear off at night for the height of it . . . the big bloomers an the wrap it round me dead tight belly flattener . . . an her wee stick insect man's eyes bulgin at the monster she's turned into.

So I laugh at that. On he goes. Shoutin out the window.

—McGinty! Show's yer long black curly teeth. Show's yer long blonde tongue. Hair all the way down her back . . . none on her head . . . just all the way down her back like a fuckin Gorilla . . . like Big Vinny wi hair. Show's yer soft wavy skin an big blue ears . . . he's goin – that was the way wi him. Laugh a minute. Jokes an patter an crazy stuff. Right mad too. Ye'd mention his name an fear would flicker across faces. An he'd greet the minute ye were nice to him. That's it . . . that's right . . . he couldn't handle niceness. He couldn't handle affection an that. He'd crumble.

A lassie he used to go out wi – she bought him a birthday cake an he gret all over it. Nearly ruined the fuckin thing. Nobody had bought him a cake an candles an a wee card an all that stuff before so he gret. An she thought he never liked the cake. So he soaks it an then kids on he's puttin it in the tumble dryer to dry. She's on the veranda listenin to sirens. Saturday night. An he's got the tumble dryer on kiddin on the cake's in there. He goes out an holds her. She says he couldn't look her in the eye cos he'd been greetin so he holds her. His arms come round her waist an they're tight an he says nothin – not a thing.

An at five in the mornin they're still there. He's got his head on her shoulder an he's holdin like it's a cliff edge an he's fallin. The stars are gone an birds are whistlin. The taxis are parked up an milk floats are out. She was head over heels so she loved it. I thought it was weird but I can understand it now.

An yet that's the same man that petrol bombed a pub. His wife comes in screamin he's up the main street stinkin of petrol. Off we go in ma Da's car. The pub's ablaze an he's launchin another bottle in. Whoosh it goes. The pub's empty. They all got to fuck out when he lobbed the first bottle. He bolts an the Polis come. They never caught him. I mean ye'd expect a shotgun mob or somethin at the door next day but not a thing. Nothin.

Bananas.

Fight the Devil. Temper like a tornado. Mad eyes. Even I was feart when his eyes went like that. An yet wi weans . . . his eyes were like a Sacred Heart picture. Caught his wife in bed. Fuckin bummer. Nobody more shocked than me when I heard what he done. The killer. Weightlifter. Kung-fu expert. Finds his wife in bed wi another guy an what does he do? What does he do? Makes them a cup of coffee. Coffee for fucksakes. I mean what the fuck's that all about? Coffee?

He comes down this day. Ye can tell he's been greetin an he's shakin like he's been on the drink. White as a fuckin sheet. He sits down;

—Caught her in bed wi some guy the day.

He's flickin through the paper not lookin up.

—Ay, right, I goes thinkin he's takin the piss. But he looks up an like an iron bar over the head. I believe him. I look out the window an he goes on.

—Ay . . . I thought there was somethin up when I kept findin shoes two sizes too wee for me at the bottom of the bed.

I laugh. He looks. I go quiet. He sighs an goes on.

—Whit a fuckin day. I comes back just after nine an chaps the door. No answer. All the venetian blinds are shut . . . the blinds I paid a grand for . . . shut tight. No answer an I'm shoutin. The house is that quiet ye know there's two people not breathin up the stairs. I goes round an tries the back door. Nothin. There's a big van up the street I've never seen before. Next thing I knows I'm on the wee roof an the window's open. I starts climbin in an the blinds are rattlin like fuck. She's appears in the room there wi her arms folded in the sexy gear I bought her. She wants to know what the fuck I think I'm playin at. I crashes on the floor in ma workin gear an steelies. She tries to block the path into the top lobby. I hears some cunt movin in the bed. Ye always know the sound of yer own bed so ye do. She still wants to know who the fuck I think I am an what the fuck am I doin in her house. I paid for that house. She folds her arms tighter but one look an she melts backwards prayin I'll only knock fuck out him an not kill him. Anyway I walks in the room an she squirms between me an him. He's lyin on the bed. An the first thing I want to know is how good lookin he is. An he's no bad. Opposite of me. Dark skin an hair, black satin boxer shorts. He's shakin uncontrollable. Black satin fuckin boxer shorts. I'm thinkin – need to get a pair of them – I looks at him. He knows me. I thinks – he's fuckin dead meat. He pisses his pants. There was no cunt more shocked than me when I never kilt him. I starts feelin sorry for him. Fuck knows how? I just says well I suppose that's that or somethin . . . I can't remember but there was this big empty silence an I went down the stairs an I don't know where it came from but I shouts up an asks if they want coffee. They must've swapped mad looks an they shout yes . . . fuckin YES PLEASE in fact. I gets the kettle on an this is the funny bit – when I opens the spoon drawer the cutlery rattles an he's up the stairs an he's thinkin . . .

KNIFE

DRAWER

KNIFE

DRAWER

. . . man he comes stumblin down the stairs an he's strugglin wi the front door. He turns round like a rabbit trapped in headlights an there's me sittin his coffee on the table. I sparks up a fag an shouts her down the stairs. They drink the coffee quick as fuck an off they go in Fernie's . . . Fernie . . . that's his name . . . his van . . . they fuck off in his van. But they never knew I only put one sugar in their coffee instead of two – they'll no fuck about wi me again in a hurry.

I gives him the she-was-a-tart-anyway, ye're-better-off-without-her routine an all that an off he pops. Seems neither up or down considerin. Considerin that's him homeless cos they had to sell the house. He's got two ex-wifes an four weans. He's got no job an he's off the drink an that.

I was sure he'd top hisself. But he never.

Four years later he's got a good job. Made. No problem. Nothin gets him down. Own house. Good bird . . .

hunky dory. We're well past givin that tart an him catchin her wi her knickers down any thought. I mean he's doin really well for hisself. That's why I don't understand it. Him hinging fae the loft an that bit paper:

NOTE NOT INCLUDED

Bunkers an Doors

Me an Stevie Gal used to play at chap-doors-run-away. We'd rattle somebody's door all night, make them really mad an then bolt the course. Clusky was mental. He used to boot ye right up the arse when he caught ye. Right on the bone.

OOH YA BASTARD!!!!

Ye were right feart of him so we chapped his the most. He'd come flyin out wi these big bulgin eyes;

—I'll get yees ya wee fuckin bastards . . . I'll get yees an I'll

fuckin kill yees . . .

he used to shout through his teeth. Me an Gal'd be scootin down the street miles away terrified but laughin.

The houses we lived in had these wee bunkers at the front. Not coal bunkers – they were just for puttin stuff in like go-chairs an that. The houses were electric.

We got this bright idea: chap his door an jump in the bunker. We were always havin bright ideas me an the Gal. This night we done it, chapped his door, booted it, flipped the letter-box up a million times, bang crash, bang crash wi the fists hammerin on the glass, punch kick, punch kick. It was like the Orange Walk goin by. Soon as we seen his shape in the lobby it was right into the cupboard.

We kept the door open enough to hear him. He comes flyin out.

Ya wee fuckin bastards I'll git yees . . .

. . . an on an on he goes wi all the usual stuff. Me an wee Gal are curled up in the cupboard, foreheads touchin, sniggerin. Gigglin away at each other as Clusky's voice disappears into the night followin his body.

Every time he'd come back after five minutes an him an Betty'd discuss all the wee bastards that lived round here need shot an whipped an it wasn't like this in our day an all this shite. They'd be goin for about five minutes. Ye could smell their posh house an see the lobby light fallin on the slabs. Me an Gal'd always wait till they shut the door an the lobby light went out an we heard the tap fillin the kettle.

(The bunker was right below the scullery sink) Then we'd explode out across the garden an Fosbury Flop the fence. We'd meet up the swingpark an laugh till

    —STEVIE . . . STEVIE!!!

or

    —DERRICK . . . DERRICK!!!

An that'd be us in for the night.

After three or four months hidin in the cupboard an Clusky shoutin the odds at the moon I got fed up.

I gets this idea so I goes to Gal,

—Gal ma man, know somethin? I'd love to see Clusky's face when he tears out the house an can't see nobody runnin up or down the lane . . . after we chap it all night . . .

Gal's noddin like a lintie. Ye can tell he sees a good idea comin. I gives him the story;

—Ye go up an rattle the door after we've been givin it a doin all night an then jump in the bunker. Clusky'll be really mad, so he will, specially if we give it extra wellie. He'll be fizzin. Foamin at the mouth. You rattle the door, flip the letter-box up an down, boot it an jump in the cupboard an when he comes flyin out the door I'll walk out ma Maw's gate as if I've just been sent for a loaf an he'll say . . . DID YE JIST SEE SOMEBODY RUNNIN AWAY FROM MA DOOR!!!!!!!!!!!!!!!!!!!?????????????

—His stupit lookin head'll be twistin this way an that way up an down the lane when he's askin me all these questions. DID YE SEE THEM RUNNIN UP OR DOWN THIS LANE!!!!!!!!!!!!!!!!!!!??????????????????????

—I'll be able to say, No mister Clusky I never seen nothin – an I'll get to see his face when he's ragin.

—HEE HEE HEE, Gal's goin an —*Rassin Fassin Rassin Fassin Rassin Fassin,* like Mutley out the Wacky

Races. So we're at Clusky's door every ten minutes this night from about seven. He's fizzin an even Mrs Clusky's been out swearin at the sky. There's no moon – just stars an Gal crawls up the lane. He climbs Clusky's fence an bellyflaps across the garden on the blind side of the door.

He stands up an I position maself at ma Maw's gate wi one hand on the post stock still, like I've been turned to stone in mid-walk. There's Gal sniggerin down wi that big grin like a half moon fell out the sky. He's sendin down his Mutley laugh now.

—*Rassin Fassin Rassin Fassin,* he's whisperin.

Ye know Clusky's near the door wi all the snibs off. Ye just know he's in the lobby in sprintin position. He's probably on his hunkers like Alf Tupper. Waitin. Snarlin like a slabbery dog. Gal knows he's in there waitin too so he gives it a quick four wi the fists, two kicks an flips the letter box wi his left hand as he's openin the bunker door wi his right. He's just in an swung the door tight wi his nails when . . .

. . . Clusky comes flyin right out onto the path screamin like a banshee.

I starts the I'm-just-walkin-up-the-lane-goin-for-a-loaf walk. His face is like a horror movie. I'm terrified. It was great. He runs at me screamin:

—YA BASTARD . . . YA BASTARD . . . DID YE SEE

SOMEBODY ... DID YE SEE SOMEBODY GOIN UP THIS LANE ... EH ... EH DID YE ... DID YE ????????

I just nods the head an goes —He's in the bunker Mr Clusky.

I've got the head tilted to one side an I'm holdin ma wrist at ma chest so as to look right innocent.

See now? I'd give a million pound to see wee Gal's face as I shouts, —He's in the bunker Mr Clusky.

I can imagine him curled up there – wide-eyed an repeatin on the silence of his lips —He's in the bunker Mr Clusky ... He's in the fuckin bunker Mr Clusky?

Clusky tears over the fence screamin like a commando an whips opens the bunker at kickin distance an starts layin three years of chap-doors run-away rage into Gal's wee curled body.

AWCH AWCH AH AH

Gal's goin an I'm laughin ma head off at the end of the lane.

—He made me do it Mr Clusky ... he made me do it ...

I can see a wee curly finger pointin out the bunker an that just makes me laugh all the more. I'm bitin ma fingers, it's that funny. Man I'm in knots, I'm doubled up, peein maself an he's still screamin at the boots goin in.

—YA WEE BOOT AWCH FUCKIN BOOT AWCHBOOT AWCH BASTARD I'LL TEACH

BOOT AWCH YE A LESSON YE'LL NEVER
BOOT AWCH FORGET . . . YE'LL NO BOOT
AWCH BE CHAPPIN ANY FUCKIN BOOT
AWCH CUNT'S FUCKIN BOOT AWCH DOOR
BOOT AWCH AGAIN BOOT AWCH

So there's me creasin maself on the cold slabs an the
stars spinnin in the water of ma eyes an Gal squealin like a
pig an Clusky goin mental wi mad delight. Never spoke to
me for ages after that, the bold Gal. His Jim gave me a doin
too but it was worth it.

The Big Empty Too

There's me an Bonzo this day down The Estate. We're on
the Mushies. Couple of joints skinned up.

    —I'm chokin Bonzo, I goes.

    The lips get dead chapped an dry on the Mushies.
Fuck me – he whips out this bottle of Lambrusco from
nowhere. They had a Christenin the day before. The day
was still bright an cos of the Mushies the wine sparkled like
mercury.

    We looked through the bottle a few times each to bend
the world. Bonzo's grinnin away at the other end of the
bottle an gettin magnified. The sky's on his head like a hat.
It felt great. Smoooooooooth.

    —Ergonomic, I kept on sayin an spinin it slow an tight

in ma hand. —Er go no mic Er go no mic Er go no mic Er
go no mic . . .

—What the fuck's erganomik?

I never answered. I kept on goin

—er go no mik er go no mic er go no mik er
go no mic er go no mik er go no mic an spinnin the
bottle slow an pressin ma skin tight. It was like the feelin of
the glass an the wine inside an the word ergonomic was the
Truth Of The Universe.

—This is a regal wine of cosmic proportion, Captain,
I goes, —a shinin nectar that needs no partakin of in the
low terrain of mud an cow slush we now traverse. This
liquid needs a special place to be consumed an you Captain
are charged wi the findin of that aforementioned place . . .

He laughed like a plastic doll his skin all bendin. I was
full of that kinda pish on the Mushies. I mind he laughed
like we were two wee boys an, for a split second, inside, I
went infra red wi happiness.

The words came pourin out like ma tongue was a page
out a book an the wind was shakin the words off. I could
see them screw their way across an twist their way into his
ears. They were words of colours an transparencies. Big
loud words had legs an arms like fat ladies an small words
looked half starved to death an scrawny like Ethiopians.
Words like blood an stuff ye could taste – they dragged
their selfs off yer tongue. Once the words had corkscrewed
in one ear, drilled themselves through his brain an crackled
out his other ear, he starts lookin serious for somewhere we
could guzzle the plonk an spark up spliffs.

Hello!

We've found it.

It's up this tree.

It's perfect.

Yer feet

are on this big branch that's twenty feet up but it's like a magnet. Ye could let go an slant back an not fall. Super glue shoes. Rooted.

No way we're fallin off this thing. There's this other branch right at

elbow size

an it's like a bar in the sky. At first it's a laugh an we do some bar-up-a-tree jokes an laugh up through the last yella leaves of autumn an the blue sky an the cold white clouds. I looks round – the colours rape into me. It's like the ecstatic cramp of orgasm in ma head an I goes,

—Shall I look back at you – autumn – in the gloamin of life an remember you rollin your golden starkness through ma scrapbook of a mind . . . shall I . . .

. . . but Bonzo placed a joint in ma mouth. Gently, like a Maw givin a wean an unexpected lollipop. Love.

—Lollipop, I starts to say. Then —Loolipop looooolipop loo ooooo ooooo ooolipop

The spliff was in ma lips an he lit it like it was somethin automatic he done a million times. A surge ran through me an I cried a bit. He never seen me. I looked the other way into the copper leaves of a maple tree.

All these things filmstriped ma head. Not black an white – brown like Victorian films an sometimes burstin wi Spielberg colour. I was cryin like waterfalls inside cos the films were all about things we never got – good dinners – the love that never came our way when we were boys. The beatings, the screamin an shoutin, the absent cuddles, (Voices in the distance.) the Da's fists. Then it all came out me in one long but quick film strip in three-D an played for Bonzo out there on a grey cloud. He watched it an right down his ear I seen the turbulence of his waterfalls all blue an foamin white an this black black water where these deep things were. An I had to look away cos Bonzo had things in him too dark to see – he'd proved that.

It was as if all the love we wanted was in the tip of that joint he placed between ma lips. I could feel his shoulder pressin close to mine an this tremendous (Voices in the distance.) warmth thrummin from him into me. We're twenty feet above the ground an a million feet above the ground.

Big black bars of silence fill the gaps between the trees.

Voices in the distance. Voices in the distance. Voices in the distance. Voices in the distance. Voices in the distance.

—D'ye think we'll still be up trees when we're eighty? he goes.

A   long   pause
I turns sorrowfully an says, —No,
an turns away. The world would drive us apart. He read all these thoughts goin round ma head like a Hotpoint number four soap sud wash.

Everythins gettin drove apart. We cling to the next thing that comes along. (Voices in the distance.) Then we're drove apart. It's you against every cunt, the whole world, no cunt wants to know. It's you against the whole sky, the universe, the whole fuckin shebang! Then it's The Big Empty. A wind made up from all the things ye hate about yerself an the world blows right through ye an all the coal fires an pieces on sausage won't warm ye. Then ye cling to somethin or somebody. Then ye're drove apart. Then The Big Empty. Then we cling. Then we're drove apart by The Big Empty. The Big Empty is what Hell's like. There's no-one there to cling to. Ye wander about inside yer own empty heart

searchin for the things ye missed out on in life. But ye'll
never find them cos ye don't know what they look like.

Voices in the distance.

—Here – have another smoke of heaven, goes Bonzo.

We laugh an kshhhhhh he cracks the cork. It goes
down ma throat ticklin like Christmas tinsel. Its light is
comin out ma nose like two torch beams an I'm searchin
the ground below.

MMMMMMMMMMMMMMMMMMM, I'm goin
makin ma best searchbeam noise.

Ma eyes shine like billiard balls. They throb out onto
some yellow an red in the trees.

Next minute I sees all these wee fellas in the trees. It's
all these elves an fairies an stuff holdin hands an dancin
round an singin a song I could understand – but the words
meant nothin. We discovered them. I nudges Bonzo.

—What? he goes.

—Elves an fairies! says I.

—So it is! he says after I point them out,

. . . so it is!!!

So we watch them come over the grassy knoll beneath
the trees an dance towards the river. Five. It's them dazzlin
red an blue Poundstretcher colours an they're happy an
they're dancin, an they're skippin. I never seen that much
happy in the one wee bit in all ma life. They can't see up
the tree an that's great. We see them at their play an they
don't know we're there.

•

But that's not what they are. They're a man an his wife an
weans. They're dancin in the grass an springin up off the

curvin daisies an every now an then the sun sends down a tube of light to wash them. The Maw an Da are smilin an sometimes they hold hands wi each other an sometimes they hold hand wi the weans. An when they think the weans aren't lookin they have a fly kiss. Me an Bonzo don't need to say nothin. We look down an we know they've not got The Big Empty. We feel like two demons now lookin out of hell down into heaven.

They don't know where hell is. The wine an the dope an the mushies an a hunger are burnin like fires in ma heart.

There's a flash an I'm transported to this place. There's rows an rows an lines an lines of people on their bellies an they've got a shoulder propped up wi a stick. Their heads tied up by their hair so they're all lookin right at me an there's pain of all sorts on their faces an under their hearts a wee fire burns an burns inflictin eternal unbearable pain.

FLASH . . . an I'm back lookin down out the tree.

They're walkin lightly, sometimes skippin. The weans are singin. One looks up the tree.

—Mammy there's two men up that tree. Look, look two men, she goes.

They angle their heads – Da mumbles an the distance between them is zero an they fold in the one bundle till they're a pile of just washed washin movin up the hill. The smiles hide, the laughter dies an the colours fade.

This rain drop's got ma face reflected in it. It hits a leaf an the leaf breaks an falls leavin aluminium tracers in the cold autumn air. The raindrop explodes sendin ma face out an out in minuscule mercury moons but fallin,

fallin.

Bonzo hands me the wine – the family scurry off an we sigh grey clouds over the comin winter.

And You Were

The gale's blowin in yer ears – so they won't hear the door shuttin. They're still laughin an jokin up in the room. Room, that's a fuckin joke so it is. Room? The door hits the wardrobe when ye open it. But there's eight in there bevvyin, all sittin on the edge of the one damp single bed. The bed is yours an hers. She puts her umbrella up every night so the water from the leakin roof runs down the wall an not onto the sixteen mouldy covers. They think ye're away to the toilet. But ye're not.

•

Ye're sittin on the edge of the bed an ye want to leave but

yer arse is welded to the sheets. Ye want to go but the aul legs are on strike so ye can't move. Ye pass the message that ye want to go an the muscles start respondin but depression takes over an ye're still welded to the fuckin bed. Can't move.

D'ye know what the last straw was? Her – that Greenock slut . . . Foggy's bird. Ye're sittin there kinda depressed. Half-cut. Carmen's flirtin wi Foggy. The jealousy's rushin through yer veins like miniature Christmas trees. Ye can't say nothin cos they'll all know ye're not so hard. Soft as fuck. If they find out they'll be right in there tearin ye apart. They can't do it physically; the fear game. Ye're mental . . . fight like fuck an all that, but right there, right in front of the bastards ye're crumblin. Cryin inside. Yer heart's enormous an empty. It's a wonder they can't hear the bells of Hell ringin inside it . . . Red. Yer skin must be red. Look at her pressin the side of her arse into him.

Ye draw the feet backwards to stand but ye're still stuck. There are no holes in the atmosphere for leavin so ye stay. Then, the Greenock slut, she get's up mid sentence – nice as ye like – lifts the skirt an drops the scants. Wi both hands she jerks herself backwards on the sink an starts pishin. No cunt flinches. Not a one. Ye can hear the pish squirtin out an runnin down the plug hole. Ye can even smell it. Ye look over. Ye can't help it. She sees ye run up the white an red of her corn-beef thighs an zero in on the dark patch. Her hands are on her legs now an they tighten an squeeze the skin. Ye think it's on purpose but ye're not sure.

Swear to God she parts the fuckin legs a bit an lifts the front of the skirt up wi her thumb. Her eyebrows go up too. They're all too blitzed to see it. She gives ye the come-up-an-fuck-me-anytime look. Her scants are below her knees an she's stretchin the elastic. They're not white like ye like them. They've been white but now they're grey. She gives ye the three teeth missin smile an bounces out the sink pullin them up, starin. She wants ye bad. Her man's got the arm round Carmen. She turns the hot well on to wash the pish away an comes over to yer bit of the bed. The smell in the room is boilin pish an stale tobacco an stinkin beer an damp bedclothes an rotten wood an a greasy aul Breville breathin away under dirty washin an the bodies heavin wi BO an Buckfast an her leg, her leg, up an down it's goin on yer thigh; up an fuckin down.

Carmen's got the arm round Foggy now. Fuck this. Ye imagine them shaggin – fuck sake what the fuck are ye doin? Ye can't help it, ye imagine them shaggin again an the Greenock slut's still rubbin the leg up an down an Carmen's eyes dart by an they're brown, brown an shinin. Her eyes are brown. Brown eyed girl. Her hair's on his shoulder. Ye want to fuckin kill him. The bastard. Does he not know who ye are? She's drawin strands of her hair out an lettin them fall like schoolgirls do when they're concentratin. But she is a fuckin schoolgirl. Sixteen! Six fuckin teen! What the fuck are ye doin here? An that's when ye stand up like ye're goin to the toilet.

•

Sneakin down the stairs ye hear slutface skulkin about in the lobby lookin for ye. She's slidin along the wall cos Marlyn took the fuse out an ye can see fuck all at night. But out the door ye go an still they're gyratin. In yer head he's on her an she's pullin at her hair like she done wi ye an she's moanin an liftin her hips up an wantin it – wantin it. Fuck sake what are ye doin to yer head?

Ye cross the empty street. Jazz gave ye the anorak. The hood blows down. So fuckin what. The rain rubs yer face an ye walk like a zombie.

No cunt'll stand in yer way.

Yer eyes are madder than night.

No cunt in their right mind's goin to pull ye up or ask where ye're goin nor nothin.

Not unless they want to fuckin die.

Not unless they want to die.

That's was it.

Die that's the answer.

Die.

In the sea.

Jump in the sea.

Ye're on the front. It's you in the middle, the sea on one side an the fuckin madness up there in that bedsit. Ye make it to South Pier an climb the gates. The South Pier – winter – empty as a mountain. No cunt for miles. Only the sea an it's shoutin. It's hissin its melancholy song an ye're goin in. Ye climb the red an yellow railin an stand.

There's two feet of board between you an oblivion. Yer hands are welded to the rail behind. Ye lean out. Yer head is over the darkness surgin below. Movin in big slow circles an it's waitin. They're waitin back at Marlyn's digs but ye can't let go. Yer hands won't let go.

—Let go cunts . . . ye say but the hands wont let go – they're not respondin. The sea is heavin up.

—Fuckin let go hand bastards . . . ye shout. The sea swallows yer voice. That's the voice in, all ye need is the rest of ye. In ye go. But the hands won't let go. The hands are in a world of their own an in the hands world they want to stay alive. Ye want to jump. Ye really want to jump. It's only the second time in yer life ye've wanted to do yersel in. Here ye are an the fuckin hands won't let go of the yella railin. The sea is waitin but it can't wait all night. It'll need to go where it goes an come back lookin for you another day.

—Let go hands – let go.

But this time ye're not orderin them. Ye're cryin cos ye can't let go an ye're beggin the hands to unclasp. But there's no fuckin way the hands are goin down that drop into the icy sea. For hours ye're jerkin forward an can't break loose. Ye end up rockin back an forwards wi the motion of the waves rollin onto the great iron pillars underneath.

Back.

An forth.

Back.

An forth.

•

The mornin light finds ye sleepin in the Windmill on the beach. Ye stare at yer hands an wonder how the fuck ye couldn't jump. If ye felt bad goin on the pier ye feel even worse this mornin. The spark for suicide is gone so ye decide to go back.

What if he's in our bed wi her sleepin enmeshed in each other – the stink of sex all over the room. The Greenock slut might even be there too in the same bed. Maybe the two of them were into her. She was like that the Greenock slut. Foggy'd bring whoever he wanted home an she'd share. Ye go to stand up but less of ye wants to go back to Marlyn's

than stay. Ye spend the day tryin to leave the Windmill.
  Back.
  An forth.
  Back.
  An forth.
  Into the light.

Into the dark.
  Into the light.

Into the dark.
  . . . but the black thoughts of them an the howlin wind stills ye.
  Ye see the evenin in starin out to sea.

The Vulcan

It was the night of ma uncle John's wake. I had a suit on an a black tie. Skrag was a boxer. Pro. Featherweight. He didn't look fuck all. This night he's up in Airdrie; bouncin. One night – twenty quid. After the Hail Marys are over an we've walked John to St Augustine's I decides to go up an see how Skrag's doin.

Me an Carmen walks in the place. First thing's the atmosphere. Cut it wi a knife. They're all sittin drinkin into the side of their mouths an lookin out the sides of narrow eyes at me an her walkin in. She's got the good togs on an I'm dressed – black suit – black tie. Skrag's at the door wi these two giant cunts, six feet big an the same round about.

The Duncansons.

Mad as fuck.

I gets her a voddy an me a Guinness an a whisky an she's talkin to Skrag at the door. Already the bouncers have horsed a few piss heads out an Skrag's done the business. We gets talkin – how's the wake an how's the bouncin an all that stuff. He's quite happy an he introduces the two fat cunts. They shake ma hand like they're tryin to break it an give me the grin. I stares them out an ye can see that the only reason they're not on me like dogs is that I'm wi Skrag an he is somebody. He's Scottish featherweight champ. Been on the telly. These cunts only know about fear an violence.

But see this night, I don't know why – the wake an the greetin an our powerlessness over dyin an all that stuff's goin through ma head an the adrenaline's squirtin in ma veins every heartbeat.

I'm at the door – I've been drinkin steady all day but in The Vulcan I've had three Guinness an three doubles. The eyes are takin on that psycho stare an ma chest's out fierce an unbeatable. I knew, even if no other cunt did that that night I was goin RIGHT ahead.

We're at this door an the bouncers are wary. They're in ma electricity an it's makin goose pimples on their skin. The hairs on their necks are like toilet brushes. Carmen's beside Skrag an he's got the arm round her. Ma mouths straight across ma face an shut except for blowin smoke out. Ye can read the bouncers' minds. They want me out.

—Skrag ye can knock aff at eleven – there's fuck all happenin the night, says one an the other nods. They were brothers an could probably read each other's minds. Carmen's all over Skrag an that gave him cred cos they were gettin more scared of ma mad stares by the minute. He's gettin the cred cos it's ma bird he's got the arm round an I'm sayin nothin. They're not psychic but they know if they flung the arm round her I'd rip their fuckin heads off – so they reckon Skrag must be right in there. The rest of the pub, all dressed up in Orange Lodge gear were givin it The Oul Orange Flute an all this stuff. Fair play to them says I.

I'm at the liable to do anythin stage now an it's quarter to eleven. The two fatties are countin down an ye can feel them easin off as the big hand swings up to eleven. Even if ma head was sayin, drive Skrag back to the Brig an get a cargo, somethin else right in the quick of me's goin wild. Ma heart starts pumpin like I've done a line of speed but I'm into fuck all drugs this night – it's booze – fuckin airline fuel.

—Right Skrag, an he hands Skrag twenty quid. Carmen's slippin her jacket on an the bouncers open the door. The cold night forces its way in an above the rooftops I mind the stars burnin like dogs' eyes.

She goes to walk out an she's pushed back by these two even bigger even fatter cunts an they stand in front of the Duncansons. I'm givin Skrag the what-the-fuck's-this-all-about look when this wee skinny dyin-off runt comes in dressed up wi big stupid lookin lapels like a seventies film cast off. His hair's dyed to fuck an his tie's loud. He's unfoldin a wad of notes an the edges of his sharp features shine in the disco lights. He's got his jacket hangin on his shoulders. Ye can just tell that he fancies hisself as some fuckin Brooklyn pimp.

One of the heavies is pressin into me like I'm nobody – like I'm nothin. The rage is whirlin up ma body an ma eyesight's wavin about. I'm holdin onto the brass rail wi one hand an I'm puttin the pint glass down easy wi the other.

The Duncansons are shitin theirselfs. Hatchet face is takin his time wavin at cunts like a God. He's been at the door at least a minute an he's still countin this dough. Fuckin thousands. He stares me in the eye but seein somethin he doesn't like he swings round an sees Skrag, the new bouncer.

—Hello, says the skinny bastard —an who might you be?

—Awright ma man, Skrag.

An Skrag sticks the hand out to shake but the prick withdraws an laughs, noddin at his men an flashin his big brown teeth. I want to crush him. I looks into the heads of his two bodyguards an instead of faces there's just these two big black fuckin holes an all this laughin comin out. Skrag's starin.

—Fuckin kill him Skrag, I'm sayin in to masel. —Kill the cunt.

I'm waitin on him layin a few lefts an rights in. The Duncansons are laughin along wi this cunt now. Carmen knows what's goin to happen an she lifts two good cider bottles, one in each hand, an lowers them down into the folds of her long black dress.

—Is this yer first night here wee man, goes the skinny bastard wearin a grin that ye wear if ye think ye're takin the cunt out somebody.

—Crush him Skrag, I'm sayin into ma teeth.

The two bodyguards think I'm tryin to talk an they nod at each other an then at me like I'm a dick. There's only seconds left. Carmen's not took her eyes off me the last twenty seconds – she's wantin to go ahead. Skrag answers.

—Ay, first night ma man.

I couldn't believe it. I'm waitin on Skrag bustin this

guy's head an he answers him back. The Bodyguards are dustin Skrag's jacket down an fixin his hair all rough like an makin him look like a right prick. It never occurred to me before but right there an then I thought that maybe Skrag was feart. Maybe his bottle was crashin. I'm searchin in his eyes an the skinny bastard says,

—It might be yer first night wee fella but it's goin to be ye last.

—Fuckin kill him Skrag!!! I goes.

Skrag's mouth drops open like he can't believe what I'm sayin.

—Kick fuck out the prick, I says without partin ma teeth.

The bouncers an the two bodyguards are lookin at me wonderin who the fuck I think I am.

—Do you know who I am? goes skinny.

—I don't give two fucks who ye are – PRICK.

Carmen moves the bottles from under her dress an blows me this kiss. The cunt's still talkin but ma temper's comin up like Auld Nick out of hell an there's no stoppin now. He's tryin to tell me who he is. I only hears one word but – MONEYLENDER. He could've called me a Fenian Bastard, called ma Maw all the cunts under the sun but that one word, that's what done him that night.

Next minute I've got the cunt an he's above ma head. I'm strong as fuck an I throws him on the dancefloor. There's plenty confusion cos his notes are flutterin everywhere an all the Orangies are whippin it in their pockets. He hits the dancefloor like a sack of spuds an the floor clears. No cunt knows what to do. They're frozen. By the time they even move I've jumped up and drove the heel into the bastard's ribs seven times.

All the time I'm ravin about . . .

Moneylender . . . fuckin moneylender . . .

Crack breakin ribs.

Moneylender . . . fuckin moneylender . . .

Crack breakin ribs.

Moneylender . . . fuckin moneylender . . .

Crack breakin ribs.

Moneylender . . . fuckin moneylender . . .

Crack breakin ribs.

Moneylender . . . fuckin moneylender . . .

Crack breakin ribs.

Moneylender . . . fuckin moneylender . . .

Crack breakin ribs.

Moneylender . . . fuckin moneylender . . .

Crack breakin ribs.

He's not movin an only eight seconds have went. I turns an the two bodyguards are only startin to move.

C'mon ya fuckin pricks!!!!!

I'm on the middle of the dancefloor an the ferocity that I laid the moneylender out has frozen all the cunts halfway out their chairs. It's always like slow motion. These two are off the startin blocks an wobblin towards me.

Crash Crash

Two well placed cider bottles an that's one on his knees. Carmen's rippin his face to shreds from the back an he's screamin like a big wean. The other cunt's runnin full tilt at me now an I sinks down about a foot, keeps the eye right on his fat beak an comes up when he's nearly on me an drives the right into his face. I could feel the shock run down ma arm an through ma body to the wooden floor.

Some birds are screamin like fuck now an we're only twelve seconds in. I'm checkin all round me now – eyes wide an mad an sayin . . .

C'MON C'MON C'MON C'MON C'MON
C'MON C'MON C'MON C'MON C'MON
C'MON C'MON C'MON C'MON C'MON
C'MON C'MON C'MON C'MON C'MON

That's when I notice Skrag's still not moved. I mean I expected him to be bangin heads. Cunts were ready to go – ye could see them gettin their birds to hold them back. But it's the usual – one wee cunt breaks loose an he's first at me across the dancefloor. Then there's hundreds of the cunts five steps behind him. I launches him an he's sprawlin on top of the moneylender.

Skrag's still not moved but the bold Carmen's launchin bottles an tumblers into the crowd. Some duck for cover behind tables an still no Skrag. I gets ma back against the bar. They're round me like a pack of fuckin dogs bootin an swipin an punchin. I'm gettin the odd blue flash but nothin too bad. I've covered up well an the stupit cunts can't get a right good swipe at me cos they're packed too close. I just kept crouchin down a foot an springin up sendin out long straight lefts an rights to a face I'd picked before I sunk. The punches were gifts – they never expected it. Down they went every time. The only thing was the barmaid's behind me an she's shoutin an greetin.

—Ya evil bastard, she's sayin over an over an smashin every fuckin spare glass in the bar over ma head. I could feel the blood runnin down. I mind thinkin that that was it. I mind thinkin I'm goin to get it here. I couldn't cover the whole thing an the cunts were shovin me along the bar sayin,

—Get the bastard in the toilet an we'll rip him open.

SKRAAAAAAAAAAAAG!!!!!!!!!

It was like he woke out a fuckin dream. —Thank fuck, says I, as he comes chargin across the dancefloor. The bodyguard that Carmen fucked wi the bottles is back on his feet an he picks Skrag up an throws him through the disco lights.

The fat bastard's smilin an lookin for applause an that takes the pressure off me a bit. This wee cunt whose been diggin me an gettin away stops concentratin an I side kick him on the knee an break his leg – stupid cunt – he's on the ground squealin like a lassie – fuckin wanker. Skrag gets back up an starts skippin towards the big cunt. The big cunt's laughin an givin it watch this – watch me annihilate this wee cunt. He never knew Skrag was a boxer. He reaches out to grab Skrag an the wee man's right in there bam bam bam bam bam bam an the fat cunts on his knees wobblin an the only thing holdin him up's his pride an Skrag fucked a few low hooks in an down he went.

Meanwhile back at the bar I'm gettin closer to the toilet an the cunts are still rainin the blows in. Skrag's crackin heads from the back an I'm crackin them from the front. But we're outnumbered. Lucky thing is that the barmaid's ran out of tumblers an so she's slappin ma head wi this soakin wet dishcloth thing an shoutin,

—Ya bastard ya bastard ya bastard, an she's greetin wi anger.

The force of them draggin me into the bog was too much an I'm strugglin to stop them. I meets this wee cunt's eyes an I can see he's evil an I can see he means to do serious damage. He's not puttin the blows in. He's standin there behind the maddies an he's lookin right in me. His eyes are dark holes in his head an he's got a hand in his pocket. I can smell the piss from the bog now an he cracks into this grin.

That's when I decides to use the blade.

I'm still takin them on the head but the blue flashes have stopped cos I'm used to it now. I drops the head down so's all the blows are hittin me on the roof. I keeps one hand up there punchin wild so's to keep them at bay. At the same time I take the blade out ma left hand pocket of ma suit jacket. It's a foldin lock blade. I opens the blade partly wi ma thumb an opens it to a click by pressin the point into ma thigh an leverin it.

The blue flashes are back again cos they're gettin free punches at me. I see the evil cunt's eyes as he opens the bog door an the orange light floods the black gaps in the writhin bodies.

They're like a pile of eels wrigglin an strong. I'm gettin weak now cos I've nearly punched masel out. I decide to stick the blade in some cunt. Any cunt. There's no way they're gettin me in that bog – they'd cut me to bits an that's that. I pulls the knife back so its heel is hard against the bar. Him wi the eyes comes closer. He's got a blade. I see it shinin in the weak toilet light. He turns to slide into the bog but he's close enough so I lunges forward wi all ma strength knowin that when I stick it to him the rest of the cunts'll shite theirselfs an bolt the course.

Honest to fuck I'm swingin the blade through the thick air of an Airdrie pub – I'm a micro second away from becomin a killer when ma head puts on the brakes. I flicks the knife away into the legs of the throng an then I notices that I saw a Polis hat bobbin through the pub.

The mob round me fell away like weans off a roundabout an I'm standin on ma own wi the stupit barmaid still slappin me wi this wet dishcloth an goin,

—It was him . . . that bastard . . . that evil bastard . . .
he started it . . . slap slap slap, she's goin an this polis is
lookin at her like she's mental.

I casually walked over to the other end of the pub. I
seen the bold Carmen crouch down to her hunkers an when
she stood up straight there was two big Whitbread bottles
left on the floor. She slides the arm round me. Skrag's
standin wi the bouncers an he's wipin blood off his face an
the barmaid's pointin at me hysterical an goin,

—That's him – him over there wi the suit on – that
bastard . . . she spits. Don't know why – she's about at least
twenty feet away an her mouth's dry wi adrenaline. This
wee Polis comes up an I thinks, oh ho here we go – lifted –
weekend in the cells, three months or more if some cunt's
got it bad up the casualty. An this is the most amazin thing
about the whole night. I mean it was just another fight in a
pub. He walks up an he grabs ma shoulder.

—I suppose you seen everythin, he goes.

An at that I sees his eyes dartin to the black tie. I'm
just about to do some explanation about how the money
lender threatened me wi a gun an all that shite when the
Polis guy walks away. Carmen looks at me. Skrag gives the
what-the-fucks-goin-on-here? look an the barmaid's dragged
off screamin by two polis women.

—It was that bastard there wi the black tie on, he's
the cunt that started it all . . . get that bastard he's evil . . .

She's makin the swear words louder than all the other
ones an there's saliva runnin down her chin now.

We spent the next two hours drinkin wi the bouncers
an Skrag an them tellin me how tough I was an me lovin
every minute an wonderin why the fuck I'm sittin there an

cunts in casualty an cunts in the cells? Carmen's listenin intently lookin at me wi a glint in her eye.

The District The Bru an The Polis Station

It's that complicated it mixes me up. I never found out why
it all happened. Everybody I met that day was mixed up as
me. It was like one of them films where the guy is caught
up in some political wrangle that he knows diddley about.

I mind I gets up that mornin an shoves on this track
suit. I'd stopped the smokin three days an I'm due up the
District for no tax disc. I decides to jog everywhere so the
fags couldn't get me back on them. Out the door I goes an
it's no a bad day so bounce bounce I goes, checkin out the
fanny up Coatdyke an along Main Street.

I gets to the court an nods at the Sikeside team an
went in quick in case they offered me a draw of their joint
an that would be me back on the fags.

It's lookin like I'm not gettin called in the mornin. I've got to sign on usually at half eleven an it's quarter to twelve. I asks Tam Boyle to listen for ma name cos I'm goin to zoom up the Bru an zoom back.

—Twenty minutes tops, I tells him.

Off ye pop an I'm zoomin up the Bru.

There's a bit of a queue so I'm standin there noddin at anybody I knew an eyein up the odd arse an thighs.

I gets to the counter expectin the usual abuse cos by this time I'm a half hour late.

I hand her the Bru card. She looks.

I'm waitin as she checks this list. I've got ma answer ready all about how I'm up the court an they're expectin me back any minute an they know I'm away up the Bru so she'd better not fuck me about. I'm gettin masel angry as fuck so I can burst out loud an mad.

She looks up an ye can tell she's not goin to shout.

—Could you stand aside, Mr Duffy, a moment. There's someone wanting to speak to you.

Faces turn at me an sweep out from the line behind. I goes to say somethin but I'm all choked up wi the angry answer. I never expected nice. I grunted fuck knows what an moved to the side.

After five minutes an me sweatin about what if they've called ma name at the court this aul biddy comes out smilin like yer granny.

—Good day Mr Duffy? she goes all nice like I'm somebody.

—Eh! Ay.

—Few questions, Mr Duffy, routine, shouldn't take too long.

Ma head's goin like fuck wonderin if I'd been caught

workin on the side or if some bastard's stuck me in for livin
wi her an her on a Monday book. I can't think what it might
be. She asks me all these stupid questions an all the time
when I'm answerin she's lookin right by me like I wasn't
there. I should've clicked there was a move on there an
then but it's always easier to see the whole shebang after it.
Another thing – she never seemed much interested in ma
answers. I mean there she is askin,

—Have you been looking for work?

—Have you had any paid work?

—Have you been offered any work?

But she's not listenin to ma answers I could've said
The Titanic as the first answer, Glasgow Celtic as the second
an Kiss ma arse as the third an she'd've noticed fuck all.
Christ lookin back now, it's a wonder I never thought I had
a parrot on ma shoulder the way she was lookin over it.
Fuckin cow!

—Right thank you very much Mr Duffy, she goes all
nice an polite an me halfway through an answer.

I stumble a few words out ma mouth as she shoves a
bit of paper under ma nose. It's the signin on bit an off she
goes. I walks off wonderin what the fuck that was all about
an two guys come up to me at the door.

—Derrick Daniel Duffy? they goes.

Right away I'm on guard cos everybody calls me Dek
even ma Maw an Da so I'm thinkin Polis or some official
bastard. A couple of wee laddies. They looked about
eighteen.

They told me they were CID. I think they were quite
surprised when I laughed an shoved them out the road. I
was strong as fuck then an there they are tryin to hold me
back by the track suit an the two of them slidin across the

shiny floor of the Bru. But what's this in the doorway? Only another two of the cunts. One's got this card an holdin it at ma face like it's a Star Trek phasor but it's the other cunt I can't take ma eyes off. He's got his hand in his jacket an I know it's a gun he's got.

—What the fuck have I done ? I'm thinkin.

There's nothin I can think of, not unless I've killed some cunt in a fight an can't remember.

Every cunt's lookin so I decides to go along easy. I know they're Polis now. I just can't figure out what they want.

Outside there's two cars full of CID. There's guys hangin about who aren't the usual ye see at the Bru. I starts to think I needs a fag. Ma mouth's dry an I'm gaspin. These two wimps have got me by an arm each an even though they look loose an light they're diggin their fingers right in. They're not deliberately tryin to hurt me the way the Polis usually do – these guys are scared. I can smell fear off them an they're treatin me like some PROVO or somethin.

—This blue Metro, says one of them like we've just left the pub an we're goin to a party an that's his motor. We piles in – me in the back wi one on each side an the other two in the front. A flash car pulls out at the front an this other one at the back an there we are like the Queen drivin along the main street. At the time ma Da's workin on a buildin site across the road an I kept hopin he never saw me.

No point askin what the fuck I'm supposed to have done. They love that. They answer back wi that silence only Polis can do. Ye end up feelin like ye've done somethin that's goin to get ye ten year.

They stick me in the interrogation room. Been there a

million times an they know it so they don't try the ye're-in-big-trouble-now-boy routine. They click the door shut quiet an leave me in the big empty silence of the room. I gets to countin the holes in the baffle board on the wall. It might sound mad but it was a right good way of gettin yer mind off the smell of disinfectant an the distant echo of heels clickin on polished floors an the jingle jangle mournin of keys turnin in door locks.

The door clicks but I stays where I am.

—Five million six hundred an twenty five thousand two hundred an sixty five – Five million six hundred an twenty five thousand two hundred an sixty six – Five million six hundred an twenty five thousand two hundred an sixty seven – Five million six hundred an twenty five thousand two hundred an SHIT ye put me off there!!!

Ever said somethin an regretted it? Well this cop's there an a woman cop an this other cunt all pigeon shit on his shoulders an the fancy hat that says if ye thought ye'd seen the highest possible rank in the polis – ye thought wrong. This guy was GOD in the Polis. Anyway he punches me one on the mouth an I flies backwards hittin the head off the bench. I mind lookin up the cops skirt for a second an I mind she caught me an then I lets out a hiss of air as the boot starts to go in an Pigeon shite's shoutin,

—So you think you're a clever bastard do you?

He's puttin the boots in an I just know it's one of them situations where he's told the other two he'll sort this bastard.

—When were you last in Blackpool?

—Eh?

BOOT

—When were you last in Blackpool?

—What are you a travel agent?

BOOT SLAP

I stares hard right through his eyes.

—And what is that supposed to mean?

—You know.

—No – clarify it for me.

I don't know why I said it. I should've kept ma big mouth shut. But I says,

—Slap me all ye want but I'll get ye – fuckin prick.

I spat on his boots. He laughs an the other two laugh. He clears his throat wi this big important throaty sound.

—An how, may I ask do you intend to GET me?

—I'll bite ma way through the fuckin walls an get ye in yer fat arse fuckin office.

The other two are laughin but I'm sharp as a tack. I can see he's scared of me. Whatever he thinks I done must be serious. But even when I'm givin him the big mad Devil stare I can see him windin his right fist for a good swipe. Christ, a cartoon's less obvious. I decides if he tries again I'm gettin in about him. Sure enough the daft cunt takes a step back. He must've been used to hittin cunts an them takin it an gettin back up for more but he never met me before.

It all happened at once. He steps back an brings up the fist. I looks him in the eye. He's got them black piggy eyes; brainless an dangerous. He must've seen the change in ma eyes. I narrowed them a bit as his fist came at me. I dodge sideways an lunge at the cunt. I throws the arms round his neck an clamp on like a vice. His fist jerks into thin air an cracks at the shoulder. I sinks the teeth into his nose an he screams like a big fuckin lassie. The other two's puttin in boots an punches but they mean fuck all on the back. Pigeon shit's screamin an I can taste blood so I squeezes the arms tighter round his head an bites further into his nose. I swear I could feel ma teeth sink in that extra millimetre. I knows the two cunts are tryin furiously to whip out the old batons so I twist round sharp so as we fall on the floor wi him on top.

—Det him off me . . . for Dod's sake Det him off me.

His voice changes cos he realises the truncheons can only be poked in ma sides from a crouched position an they're not doin damage. Despair creeps into his voice.

—Oh ma Dod det this madman off me.

The door's tryin to open but it can't cos it's bangin off Pigeon shite's head. Whoever's behind it's not givin up, they're puttin their weight behind it an – BANG – Pigeon Shite's out like a light an his dead weight flops on ma body. The rest of them get a fright an next thing I knows I'm on ma own an there's shoutin an bawlin about madmen an ambulances out in the polished floor an disinfectant department.

I'm in the cell an an hour's passed. This plain clothes guy comes in an asks ma name. I tells him. He asks me if I ever owned a silver Volkswagen Passat estate. I says I never even seen one, (which was a lie cos Big John had one an he was in Blackpool an come to think of it he seemed to be a bit flush these days an then it all clicked thegether. That big cunt had done it since we were boys. He's gave ma name to anyone who asked him for his name an address. He probably registered the car in ma name an then done a robbery an here's me gettin the blame. Big fuckin bastard, I says.) He asks me where I was on March 14th. Lucky it was black Friday in March an I'm superstitious an I tells him I was in the fuckin cells for breach. He goes away expectin to find out I'm a liar.

He comes back an says that's right enough an goes away bitin his bottom lip.

Ten minutes I'm wonderin what it's all about an in comes Pigeon shite wi this plaster on his nose. I jumps on the table an gets ready. What does he do but stand in the doorway wavin me out wi his arm. I smell a rat. Never trust a Polis, is what ma Granny used to say. I expect a team out in shiny floor territory so I springs out in Kung Fu position ready to get done in. No cunt. Pigeon shite mumbles,

—You're free to go. You'll be happy to know we're not goin to charge you this time.

I should've went mental an shouted about wrongful arrest but his nose gave me some satisfaction so I give him all about how I just left the court an what if they called ma name an I wasn't there.

Five minutes later I'm in the back of a Sherpa on the way back to court. The one I was goin to jog back to after signin on. I beg a fag off a cop an puff away wonderin what the fuck that was all about. They take me round the back an into the cells. I never seen anybody comin up out of custody in the District court except for maybe the odd drunk. But there I am in the cells at the bottom of the court.

An the Polis are still not givin up. Big John must've been spotted in Blackpool cos the Polis obviously thought that I wasn't me an Big John was – or somethin – fuck knows. Up comes this screw,

—You're not Derrick Duffy – I've lifted him a few times.

I nods side to side an says —fuck off mate I've had enough o this shite.

He walks away. So John's been lifted an had his photo an dabs took an gave ma name – the bastard.

I hears ma name from the court an they come an open the cell. Ye should've seen Tam Boyle's face when I comes out custody cos he knew I was only up for no tax. There was cunts leavin the court left right an centre cos they thought the beak was in a bad mood.

I got a twenty five pound fine cos the JP never knew what was goin on either. Big John denied it all. I still can't understand it. I jogged home smokin a fag decidin to stop another day.

Our Lady of the Carmels

I mind this time years ago we were rushin back from Kirk Street in the rain. I looks up an the clouds are rollin over the roofs that fast it's like the houses are rushin through the sky. It was me, ma Maw, an a load of weans, some in the pram, some hangin off the pram an some walkin. We were gettin soaked so we goes into St Augustine's an stands out the rain in the doorway. Three of us bumped the pram up. Silver Cross – a battleship an the rain made the hood an cover shine like leather. Whoever was in it was kickin up bumps an splashin water drops onto the shinin chrome. The pram looked alive. A monster on wheels.

We all pressed round ma Maw's legs. The wind blew her head scarf an the rain ran down her skin. I mind her skin was white. Definitely white. She's lookin at the clouds an her top teeth are bitin her bottom lip. It's like she can read somethin in them we can't.

—Won't be long, she goes. —Just a shower.

An she's still lookin up like she's scared. Like somethin's gonnae come right out that sky an bite off our heads. She walks the pram sideways up to the wood of the door. The wind crushes round the corner – whistlin an growlin like the Devil. This cold spins up ma back an I drag air in through ma chatterin teeth. I imagin I'm in the North Pole on an expedition an the weans are all huskies an the pram's a sledge an ma Maw's a polar bear. Her hand comes down softly on ma head an flattens ma hair forward. She feels ma temperature. Funny thing was . . .there I am freezin to death an her hand feels cold on ma head.

—Ye're still not well, son, she goes, —It'll be yer bed wi plenty to drink the night . . . if God spares ye.

She said that all the time, about God sparin ye an all that. I'm thinkin that God's right there wonderin if he was goin to spare me or not. I stared into the flowers on her dress; big red an yellow things. Our Linda's hair came whippin round in a gust of wind an hit me. I turns an she's grippin ma Maw's dress snotterin an shiverin into it. Ma Maw looks down an pulls Linda into her. Whoever it was in the pram is kickin up the covers an roarin. Linda starts all this,

—I'm freezin Mammy . . . I want to go ho . . . ome . . .

—Right right, ma Maw's goin lookin round an the rain's gettin heavier an the wind's gettin bigger an the clouds are mad. She looks at me. I mind maself reflected in the watery blue of her eyes.

—Away in there son an pray that it'll stop rainin.

I looks at her.

—In there?

The door opens an bangs like magic.

—What'll I say?

—Prayers that the rain'll stop.

I squeeze in behind the pram an I'm halfway through the door when she says,

—An mind an sit near the heaters when ye're sayin yer prayers. What have ye to do?

—Say ma prayers.

—What for?

—For no rainin?

—And where have ye to sit?

—Down the front.

—Down the front near what?

—The altar?

—No . . . a heater.

—A heater?

—Ay. Tell the priest yer mother's out here if he sees ye.

I slid into the warm quiet. Ma feet clicked on the floor an ye could hear the rain batterin the roof an the colour windows. It was like a big bit of quiet was caught in by the big walls an high roof. The candles burnt away at the other end like crushed stars an there was a red one up in the altar makin itself into criss-cross lines cos ma eyes were full of rain.

Right down the front I goes spinnin round as I walked. Ma mouth's wide takin in big quiet breaths. Never been in a chapel on ma own before. I felt better right away cos of the smell of some snuffin candles. I got right to the altar an the steam's risin off me. If anyone saw me they'd've thought

I was a ghost appearin in mist at the candles.

I lit a candle an stuck ma hands thegether an started to pray.

—Hail Mary full of grace the lord is wi thee blessed art thou among woman an . . .

On an on I'm goin an I mind how I knew the prayers an how to kneel there wi the back straight an the hands thegether an flat so I suppose I must've been at school an they showed me what to do. But I couldn't say the prayers right cos there was a big heater an it was makin me dizzy. I closed ma eyes to stop from fallin onto the spinnin marble.

—Hail Mary . . .

•

I come out the door an the first thing to hit me is ma Maw's face. Her eyes look like two holes bored through to the blue sky behind her head. Her mouth opens an the sunlight flashes on her teeth. Steam's risin from the ground an the rest of the weans are already bumpin the pram down the stairs. Her face changes cos I'm eatin a penny caramel an I've got one held tight in each hand. At that time penny caramels were the size of shoe boxes. She asks what I'm eatin an I says,

—*Mmmmmchchchchmmmmmmmshlp.*

She prises open ma left hand an all the other weans are starin through the sunlight at ma chewin mouth. The green an white an red of the caramel wrapper is peekin out ma skin.

I want	I want	I want	
	I want	I want	I want
I want	I want	I want	I want

I want
   I want I want I want I want
 I want I want   I want I want
    I want

is all ye can hear an the wean in the pram poked the top of its head over the rain cover – swear!

I chewed like mad till there was enough room in ma mouth for the caramel an some words.

—Our Lady gave me them.

—What?

—Our Lady . . . she gave me them.

—Our Lady? What d'ye mean Our Lady?

She sticks her fists on her hips an shoves one leg out. I've seen that position before so I know she means business. I chew furious an make more room for more words. I swallow a big chunk of sweet saliva.

—Our Lady . . . she . . . she was up the altar . . . she she . . . gave me them.

All the eyes an ears have gathered an the wean in the pram is still as a doll, listenin. Ma Maw looks up at the sky an then, lettin out a long breath, goes,

—An what did she look like this . . . Our Lady?

By this time I've only got the wee bit of the caramel left that tastes like salt an they're tryin to open ma finger to get at the other ones.

—She . . . she came down off the altar . . .

—Jesus . . . Ma Maw shakes her head.

—I was prayin on the kneely bit . . . blue she was – all blue.

—Jesus Christ . . .

—It was Hail Marys an Our Fathers . . . an a candle . . . I lut a candle . . . an an . . . an . . . I looked up . . . an this Lady . . .

Oh Jesus Mary an Joseph . . .

All the weans were starin at me, then ma Maw, an then me again.

—What did she look like son? goes ma Maw reachin out an feelin the temperature of ma head again.

—She . . . she was all dressed in blue an an she . . . she . . . floated . . . down . . . an . . . an she said, why are ye here my son? An I said I'm prayin that it'll stop rainin for ma Mammy an ma sisters out there.

—Oh! Jesus Mary an Joseph bless us an save us, he's dyin . . . I knew I shouldn't've took him out in this weather.

She gets me by the shoulders an crouches down so her eyes are right into mine. All the weans come in close so that we're like a secret circle.

—Tell me son . . . tell me what she looked like . . .

—All blue . . . she appeared out of nowhere . . . she was all blue an she floated over . . . the candles were burnin an they were blowin in the wind an there was no wind but they were still blowin . . . an I was sayin the prayers like ye said an she said what are ye prayin for son an I said that it'll stop rainin for me an ma mammy an ma sisters an the wean an she said go now an ye'll find that the rain has stopped an the sun is shinin an I bowed an said thank you Our Lady an genuflected an she smiled this big giant smile an an an . . . I got up an I starts walkin out . . . an the candles are flickerin . . . an some are snuffin out . . . an . . . an . . . she shouts Hoy You! An I spins round an she floats over an stuffs three penny caramels in ma hand an then she floated away an the candles flickered some more an she disappeared.

—Jesus preserve us, I've got a saint on ma hands here. So there's ma Maw blessin herself an givin it all this holy stuff an all the weans have got long amazed faces on an the wean in the pram stunned to a lump of wood an the sky is blue, definitely blue. The rain has definitely stopped an the sun is surely shinin on us. We're a pool of light an amazement an me chewin away on the second holy caramel when . . .

AAAAHHHHHHHHHHH
JESUSMARYNJOSEPH

There's ma Maw wavin her hands in front of her face cos the door's openin an this face is appearin.

—Oh Hello Alice, goes the face an the body steps out.

—Jist out for a wee fag hen.

All the weans are on their knees spoutin Hail Mary's like a fountain. Ma Maw lets out this loud laugh an its ribbon of echo is snipped off by the closin door. The cleaner reaches into her blue overall pockets an gets the fags out. She gives one to ma Maw. They light up an the smoke floats up into the blue sky. The rest of the weans are amazed at two things.

1. How our Maw knows Our Lady so well.

2. That Our Lady smokes Senior Service same as ma Maw.

Skid Row

Skid Row's not a place, it's a state of mind. That's why when ye hit it, ye're a goner, there's no turnin back. Who's goin to accept ye've hit Skid Row if ye're still doin ordinary things like workin an stuff? No cunt – that's who. Most cunts'll say ye've got a dose of the Poor Me's.

But ye've gave up an that's that. There's no energy in the statement, in fact there's no statement, there's only the acceptance of watchin the last drains of self worth trickle out eyes that are finished. Ye've had enough; no point in whimperin.

It's more than yer existential dread . . . it's past the point of thinkin an feelin. It's wantin the temporary death of oblivion; too dead yerself to go to death so ye wait. An ye wait. Ye might get it crossin the road not lookin like ye always do. Or the young team might do ye a favour an stick ye wi a blade or crush yer head wi a baseball bat. It's all irrelevant. It's nothin like the Poor Me's cos there ye're lookin for a perverted comfort, like a wean wi its thumb in its mouth. But this time there's no comfort wanted. It's blackness ye want; the engulfin nature ye suppose death to be. The paradox is that the spark, the tiny light, needed to do yerself in; that wee bit of self propulsion, is gone long time ago.

That's why ye're at the wall for the umpteenth time lookin into the canal. Twenty, maybe thirty feet down. If ye could climb the wall, (it's only five feet) ye wouldn't need to jump. Ye'd just topple easy over; keep the hands in the pockets an move ten metres a second squared into the flat black expanse.

There's no way ye'd struggle. Even the breath would be slow an rhythmical suckin in two maybe three gallons of water cold on the inside of the lungs. Ye'd taste it wi indifference, bitter, an ye'd sink like all the others that's flung theirselfs in.

Ye'd float up soon enough provided ye never got snagged on the weeds or an aul pram or a burnt out car in the murky water wi the current foldin in an out the slow swingin doors. A wean maybe, or some aul guy might find ye an get a shock but what can ye do about it? Ye're even less in control after ye die.

Ye're at the wall. Not back to the wall . . . not clichés an provokin statements . . . there's been enough of them over the years. There's been all the drama an the violence an sex an some success. Some success. Then the sting of failure after failure an the ghostly tumble down till ye burst through what ye thought was the bottom. Till nothin matterin doesn't matter.

So ye're at the wall an if ye were on the wall . . . on the copin stone at the top . . . a wind could blow ye over. If there were stairs or somethin ye could shuffle up them an over ye go. If the wall wasn't there perhaps? One step into the wind would do the trick.

But what if there's someone under there drinkin wine. They'll see the splash an shout an get a fright. If it was the young team they'd pretend not to be scared an shout abuse an laugh as ye died. They might even chuck a few bricks for good measure.

—Die, ya aul cunt! they'll shout an call ye Flipper an Kermit the frog an all this stuff. But the laughter would skite over the surface an scatter in the dark trees. Seein people die was easy. Laughin at them dyin was easy too . . . but livin wi it – that's the hard bit. That's the baggage that's too heavy. Ay yer muscles get strong cos ye're young an ye've got the hormones but what when they deteriorate an the weight ye've got to carry's still the same or heavier? What happens then? They won't think of that, the young team when they're hurlin the bricks an laughin.

They'll only feel their future in that wee silent pause when they realise ye're dead. An what if some of them's cracked yer skull wi one of the bricks?

Murder case.

After the silent pause they'll laugh again but this laugh'll be different.

Empty.

Hollow.

The fear'll be stickin through like the spokes of a burst bike wheel in a plastic poke.

If none of them get ye wi a brick, it'll be, —get the polis an tell them some aul cunt's committed Sunnyside off the bridge.

If a brick gets ye they'll shuffle away sayin the usual stuff that they say so that somethin can be said. They'll not say what they mean cos each an every man'll think that they are the only ones who know who done the murder an they can't deal wi it so it's all . . . someone else'll find him floatin by the farm or down Bargeddie way in the mornin. We weren't here the night.

Off to the dancin an shaggin some bird they'll go. In the mornin when it starts to piece thegether they'll never be the same again. Oh they'll be silent an they'll drift away from each other but they won't forget. One day that weight'll take them to the same wall. Skid Row's not a place; it's a state of mind.

So ye're at the wall. Cars are rushin by. Mostly taxis. Ye can smell the young birds inside. Curly hair an shinin lips mean nothin. They're smilin at nothin an flickin their heads back an laughin. The don't even know ye. Yours was another age, another set of dreams an, yet, the same aul wall an the same aul canal. There's a queue for this wall an the distance between the people is measured in time but it's still a queue. The last taxi had one that looked like Carmen an ye remember that day.

—Where are you goin? she shouts.

—Where d'ye think I'm goin!

—If you're goin where I think you think ye're goin then ye're goin to end up where ye know ye'll end up so where the fuck do you think ye're goin?

—Where do you think I'm fuckin goin . . . ya bastard?

—Fuckin go then – go, ye know what'll happen.

Ye might have no feelins now but ye had them all then. Ye walked away from the door. The weans were peepin out the blinds like they always done. Fear – that's what ye left them, fuckin fear. Ye done the guilt bit over them, now that was even gone.

It was the pub that night – there was a big cold through yer middle – a big fear an somehow ye knew that was the last door she'd ever slam on ye.

Fuck knows how ye got to here. It's all foggy now but down an down ye went. Ye started in The Hotel that night an ended up in the Pop but that was ten years ago. Ten fuckin years. Where did ye go? Everywhere, that's where. The only thing different was the view. Blackpool, London, France all them places where people like you go. But ye could fight then. Ye were good at the fear game. Ye could roll into a ball when the boots were goin in an spring back up an lash out like a maniac. Basic survival. That went too – two, maybe three years ago. Or was it days, or was it months? It wasn't a bolt of lightenin or fireworks nor nothin. It was more like a gigantic sand-glass that frittered away till there was none left. Ye were empty an the world could see right through ye an all the philosophy couldn't save ye.

Oblivion.

Drink.

So ye take a good slug of El Dee. The whites of yer eyes swivel an ye wonder who's lookin at ye. Ye can feel them behind but ye don't turn round. So long as they don't want the wine. So long as they want anythin but the wine. They can have yer body. That's even happened. No problem. The young team would reach that too, some of them. Some big hairy bastard'll shag them an they'll accept it. They'll fill up wi hate but they won't do nothin. They'll repress it all. They might do it for fear or they might do it for money. The figure moves an ye see it's some skinny cunt.

—See's fuckin drink!

The knife's diggin in yer ribs an ye laugh; more like a grunt. Ye laugh – so he laughs an ye see his missin teeth. He's not in Skid Row yet cos he's got a knife an he's stickin it in yer ribs, that's how he's not in Skid Row, that's how ye know. No cunt in Skid Row sticks someone wi a knife – ye need hormones for that. But he notices ye've got no fear. In Skid Row the fear's gone. He takes the knife away an reaches inside yer coat. Ye let him take the bottle. Ye know he's comin to Skid Row an the knife's comin to his ribs so ye laugh. He thinks ye're mad an takes a step away an laughs back wi big wide eyes swivellin between swigs.

Ye showed no fear. He mistakes it for bravery an gives ye the wine back. He grunts a cigarette under yer nose an scorches a match off the wall. In the hellish flame ye recognise him. So ye went to school thegether? So what? He thinks ye don't see who he once was so he lights yer fag, an his, an turns his face to the darkness.

He's a couple of steps closer to Skid Row now an he feels the jolt. He stands there cos he thinks ye don't know him. Ye can feel his hand in yer pocket but that's nothin – nothin compared to the dead men's pockets you've searched. He moves to yer other side an ye laugh again. He thinks ye're away wi the fairies an this time he stuffs his arm right in. He rifles all yer pockets. Ye're not reactin. It's like sexual assault. That's what ye're just thinkin when he pulls yer zip apart an gets his hand on yer dick.

Ye don't flinch. He starts wankin ye. Hard on's ye haven't had for a long time. No hormones. Ye let him fiddle an his breath's hot on yer neck. He's got it right out now an there's cars goin by but yer elbows are restin on the wall an ye blow smoke into the cold air sittin above the canal. Ye try an imagine this is a woman doin her stuff just to see what happens. But there's not a spark of arousal. He's obviously got the same idea an he's ticklin yer arse hopin that will sort ye out.

Ye flick the fag down, down, into the canal an out it hisses. He's carried away now an sticks another fag in yer mouth an gives ye a light.

Yer trousers fall to yer ankles an there's cars goin by. No pants – shat them an threw them away two or maybe three days ago. Or was it years? The canal's shovin its way westwards an then he's on his knees an he's got it in his mouth an he's slobberin away there like a dog an there's cars goin by. Cars goin by. Ye can hear them an ye can hear their brakes as some of them slow down to see what the fuck's goin on.

He slabberin away there an goin, —Dy'e like it baby? D'ye love it Darlin? . . . an it's floppin in an out his mouth an there's no reaction. That doesn't put him off,

—Shag me baby! . . . he's goin now an he's grabbin yer hips an makin them sway in an out. Cars are brakin as they go by. Ye know they're sayin look at them aul perverts an all that stuff but ye let him carry on suckin. There's nothin else to do. He slaps yer arse quick an sharp. —Get fuckin hard ya bastard or I'll stick ye.

Ye notice that all this time he's been wankin hisself an suckin yer cock at the same time. He needs ye to get hard for his own gratification so he stops wankin hisself an works his finger up yer arse. Ye can feel his long nail on yer intestines. Ye don't react an he's shovin it in an out. A swan flies up the canal an then another. The fog's curlin up on the edges of their wings. An there's a noise. A woosh like angels' wings used to make in the films. Woosh woosh an off to heaven. The swans are white, that's all they are – white in the blackness.

—I'm goin to shove it up yer hole, tart . . . ye hear me, tart tart . . . he keeps sayin over an over. It's turnin him on to say tart tart all the time. He gets behind ye an tries to force ye to bend over a bit. Ye put yer forehead on the cold wall. He's tryin to get his semi up yer arse but it's not hard enough, his hormones are too low. He's gettin nearer Skid Row all the time. Ye suppose he knew he couldn't get solid an that's why he wanted you hard so ye could shag him. He was far removed from your reality if he thought that. Ye sense him gettin angry an he spins ye round.

Cars are goin by real slow. Their lights glitter on his knife.

He pushes the knife forward an, holdin yer cock like an elastic band, he cuts it off. That's it – he cuts off yer cock an the blood splashes out onto the pavement. A passin car screams an ye look at the blood. Ye decide that bleedin to death's OK. He laughs an throws the cock in the canal. Weird, ye hear its little splash an imagine a big pike snappin it up before it sinks to the bottom.

That act that will take him to Skid Row. It's the rules of Hell – the more heinous the act the quicker ye get there. The look on his face ye recognise. But somethin is happenin. Ye turn an by some miracle ye want to try to climb the wall. The blood's drainin out fast but ye try to swing a leg over the wall. He sees what ye're doin an does up his trousers. Wi his bloody hands he pushes ye up. Christ! Ye're on the wall at last. Ye're naked from the waist down like them dreams that used to embarrass ye. Blood is runnin down both thighs an cars have piled up to watch. He throws the knife over an walks into the dark trees. Ye know he's goin to Skid Row but he doesn't. He still believes men can forget. The only thing they forget is that they can't forget. The blue light flashes in the distance. There's the drip drip of yer blood, oily, on the surface of the canal. A branch twitches. A slight wind catches ye an ye're fallin.

F

A

L

L

I

N

The Dummy

The Dummy left the scheme. I thought he liked it here but he left all of a sudden. Him an his wife. Here today gone tomorrow.

—The Dummy's wife tied her hair back tight so she looked like it was trapped in a phone box an she was walkin away, says ma Maw this day in aul Mary's house.

Mary's ih hi'n away there like she's listenin an she's got this mad grin on her face but ye can tell her head's away.

—Remember Mother? says ma Maw an Mary nods. Ma Maw goes on wi the story.

—I was about eight, she goes, . . . an the Dummy came to the door wi these plants.

—Oh hi yi, I says an the Dummy handed me a cardboard box.

—UG UG UG, he's sayin an noddin at the garden.

Ma Da had just dug bits of it up at the weekend so I knew the plants were for that bit. He was quite handsome, the Dummy. I smiles at him sayin right right all the time so he knew I knew what he was on about.

•

Mary's noddin the head an her eyes are glassed like she was right there. A smile appears an ye can tell they were happy times. An another thing. I know this sounds mad – it wasn't the story about the Dummy she was listenin to. I mean she knew the story about the Dummy. The bits aul Mary liked was the bits about Danny diggin the garden. Her eyes were shinin for Danny slidin the edge of the spade in the dirt an shovin it down to the lug. She never gave two fucks for the Dummy an the plants an ma Maw's story. But I did. I'm listenin about the Dummy wi ma ears an watchin a different story on ma Granny's eye surfaces.

So ma Maw's still on about the plants for the garden.

•

The Dummy walked away backwards an stumblin starin at me. I stood at the door smilin like an idiot an noddin till it was just his head bobbin up an down behind the hedge. I sticks the plants on the scullery table an forgets about them till ma Da comes in.

—Oh my Christ is this what's for ma tea the night? he shouts.

I goes in an he's tryin to eat the plants wi a knife an fork.

—Remind me to tell yer Maw never to let ye make the dinner again, Alice from the palace, he says an stuffs some leaves into his mouth.

—No NO Da, I goes, they're not the dinner – the Dummy brung them in – he says they're for yer front garden.

Right away he's on his knees in prayin position.

—My Christ the Dummy can talk now, he's goin.
—It's a miracle, ma wee lassie seen a miracle. We shoulda called her Bernadette right enough. Hey Mary, he shouts, —Alice from the palace heard the Dummy talkin the day, it's a miracle. Get the rosary beads out.

All the time I'm tryin to tell him that the Dummy can't talk. I never wanted him goin out in the street an shoutin that the Dummy can talk.

—It's a miracle, get the candles out an get the priest round an fill him to the top lip wi whisky, – an all this stuff cos that's the stuff that he always done. Every time I went —No Da it was . . . he'd butt right in goin, —Oh don't talk to me ye're too holy – away to the convent. Mary Mary – away up on that bus an bring Sister Mary Bridget down here to measure this halo round wee Alice's head.

An he stares up at this halo. I tries to grab it an he's goin, —Oh Oh Mary she's tryin to touch her halo, tell her – Don't put yer hands near that halo hen – it'll burn the fingers right off ye.

I ran to the lobby mirror an there it was. Dim, but it was there this halo. I felt like a cheater cos there was no miracle – the Dummy couldn't talk at all. I was about to burst out greetin wi all the fuss when the door goes. The door swings open an there's the Dummy. He's grinnin.

—Ooh OOH, he shouts.

Ma Da shouts Right! from the scullery an out he goes.
The two of them go in the garden an talk like demented
windmills. The Dummy goes away an in comes ma Da.

—Hey Mary, he shouts, —this one's not too hot at
the aul miracles. The Dummy's lost his voice again.

He looks at me an sure enough in the mirror the halo
popped like a cartoon.

•

Mary's still glazed over an smilin. She's rememberin the
crack she had wi Danny. She's laughin out loud inside her
head. Her body's old an fadin but inside, she's young an
her man's in from work an kiddin the weans. Alice carries
on.

•

—Ay. Me an ma pals were out there one summer. Ropes
an peever. Right outside the Dummy's window. We thought
nothin of it when this big lorry comes up the street. It stops
at the Dummy's an we had to move up a bit. These men
start carryin the Dummy's stuff into the van.

—Oh look at all the lovely stuff the Dummy's got,
we're all goin an stood there mesmerised at the radiogram,
the nice tables an chairs – it was a palace bein emptied.
The Dummy an his wife had no weans. Ye could smell
flowery furniture polish an the tang of the pine. It was like
the furniture was wearin perfume. For two hours we
watched the cooker, the couch, the piano, the beautiful four
poster bed an then the carpets an curtains. The only thing
left was the wallpaper.

—When we went home for our dinner the talk must have been how the Dummy had the best furniture ye ever seen. Nicer than in the chapel even. But nobody listened. Well nobody listened till the Dummy an his wife came home. They went to Glasgow every week to this place for Dummies to learn other Dummies to talk wi their hands. I always wished I could talk wi ma hands but they moved. Well, know how they never listen to weans?

—We're out on the street an every Maw in the scheme shouted on her weans at the same time. The Polis arrived in all sorts of cars an vans an ploddin. The place was buzzin. We thought the Dummy was flittin but it was a robbery. Somebody had robbed his house.

—Lucky we were there, I thought cos we described every bit of furniture an bedcovers down to the last nail an stitch but could we tell them the number of the van? No. The colour of the van? No. What the men looked like? No. How many men? No. We were useless – the Dummy was stripped bare. Gutted. We had a whip round an the Dummy was supposed to have a right few bob. So. Soon all this other beautiful lookin furniture made its way in his house along wi a big crazy collie called Ug Ug. That's when I says to maself I'd make sure when I saw anythin suspicious I'd remember the people best an not the stuff that's happenin.

•

I'm pissin maself laughin an Mary's rockin back in her chair laughin silent. Our Donna's on the floor almost wettin herself an Alice goes on wi the story.

—That's not the half of it, she goes.

—Years later. I'm thirteen – a wummin nearly – there's a prowler about the scheme. He interfered wi the lassies that work in the chippy an the pictures comin up the gas close. He used to peep in windows too. He's been chased a couple of times but never caught.

This night I hears screamin from Isa's across the street. There's Isa hangin out the window shoutin rape rape – she was about twelve an if she was raped it must've been through the window cos a boyfriend couldn't get a hundred yards near the front door for her aul rosary-beaded Maw, never mind a mad-eyed rapist. I runs into the street an I sees this big skinny guy boltin up the backs. He's got starin eyes an they look white, like there's no colour bits in them. The backs went all the way up to the railway then. I'm tryin to make out a description of this guy when someone grabbed me – well – ma heart was in ma mouth. I turns weak an shakin an it's the Dummy.

—That way . . . he went that way, I points, an the Dummy runs up the backs. He catches the guy an I hears punches an gruntin an branches breakin an I sees this guy clamberin the fence kickin the Dummy on the face. The Dummy's holdin the guys leg to stop him gettin to the railway where no-one could find ye.

This team of men come pourin past me. I could smell the drink an that steelwork smell ye don't get anymore. They disturb the Dummy an the big skinny guy disappears over the fence leavin the Dummy tryin to point out what's happenin. But it was only me that seen the guy disappearin over the fence cos the men set about the Dummy an he squealt like pig an the steel toed boots went in an in an in an I'm shoutin, —It wasn't him, it was this big skinny guy . . . leave him leave him. It wasn't him, it was this big skinny guy . . .

. . . an I can see the Dummy's dark eyes pleadin in

the mesh of darkness an grass an shinin steel boots an grunts an men callin him all the fuckin perverts. I fainted. When I came to the Dummy was in hospital. The next week I'm out on the street on ma own an there's the Dummy an this other big lorry an all his new nice furniture gettin loaded on.

　—The Dummy an his wife came up their path trailin the mad dog. People were peekin out doors an curtains. The street was quiet as Christmas. I was leanin on the railins. The Dummy's wife spat on the street before she climbed in the lorry. The lorry drove a couple of feet an stopped. I was cryin. Just then the Dummy gets out the lorry an walks up to me. He runs his fingers in ma hair. He bends over an kisses the top of ma head. He smiles an turns. The van turnin out the street was the last I ever seen of the Dummy.